Harlequin Presents and bestselling author Charlotte Lamb welcome you to the world of Barbary Wharf.

In this fascinating saga, you'll experience all the intrigue and glamour of the international world of journalism. You'll watch the inner workings of a newsroom, share the secrets discussed behind closed doors, travel to the most thrilling cities in the world. Join the players in this high-stakes game as they gamble for the biggest prize of all—true love.

You've met Nick Caspian and Gina Tyrrell, whose dramatic story of passion and heartache unfolds throughout this series. You've watched as many of their friends and colleagues at the *Sentinel* met and fell in love. Now the spotlight is firmly fixed on Nick and Gina—their turbulent relationship has reached its final crisis. But will this battle bring them together, or will it completely tear them apart?

Don't miss these unforgettable romantic adventures each month in Harlequin Presents—the bestselling romance fiction series in the world.

The Editors

THE SENTINEL

NICK CASPIAN SHOT

LONDON—Nick Caspian, joint owner of the *Sentinel*, was shot last night while leaving the Barbary Wharf complex. A hospital spokesperson has confirmed that Mr. Caspian is under observation and that his family is by his side.

Police are questioning a number of known gang members in London's East End in relation to the shooting. Sources claim Mr. Caspian has received numerous death threats over the past few months in response to a series of articles published by the *Sentinel* on the increase in gang violence within the city.

Investigators are not, however, ruling out a possible link between the attack on Mr. Caspian and rumors of a corporate takeover at the *Sentinel*. Mr. Caspian's controlling interest in the paper, and therefore his editorial control, are reportedly being threatened.

TAMAKI MAKES PLAY FOR THE *SENTINEL*

LONDON—A Japanese newspaper magnate, with extensive publishing holdings in the United States, is rumored to be engineering a takeover at the *Sentinel*, one of London's oldest daily newspapers. Mr. Tamaki has made his interest in the paper well-known within the business and media community.

Mr. Tamaki's interest has been heightened, sources claim, by his daughter's recent engagement to Philip Slade, one of the *Sentinel*'s major shareholders. Slade's shares and his own business savvy may help Mr. Tamaki realize his daughter's well-publicized dream of running a major newspaper. However, in order to succeed, he will have to acquire a contolling interest in the *Sentinel* from one of its two majority shareholders, Gina Tyrrell or Nick Caspian.

Sources at the *Sentinel* refused to comment on the rumored takeover.

Charlotte Lamb

Surrender

BARBARY WHARF

Harlequin Books

TORONTO • NEW YORK • LONDON
AMSTERDAM • PARIS • SYDNEY • HAMBURG
STOCKHOLM • ATHENS • TOKYO • MILAN
MADRID • WARSAW • BUDAPEST • AUCKLAND

If you purchased this book without a cover you should be aware
that this book is stolen property. It was reported as "unsold and
destroyed" to the publisher, and neither the author nor the
publisher has received any payment for this "stripped book."

Harlequin Presents first edition March 1993
ISBN 0-373-11540-7

Original hardcover edition published in 1992
by Mills & Boon Limited

SURRENDER

Copyright © 1992 by Charlotte Lamb. All rights reserved.
Except for use in any review, the reproduction or utilization
of this work in whole or in part in any form by any electronic,
mechanical or other means, now known or hereafter invented,
including xerography, photocopying and recording,
or in any information storage or retrieval system, is forbidden without
the permission of the publisher, Harlequin Enterprises Limited,
225 Duncan Mill Road, Don Mills, Ontario, Canada M3B 3K9.

All the characters in this book have no existence outside the
imagination of the author and have no relation whatsoever to
anyone bearing the same name or names. They are not even
distantly inspired by any individual known or unknown to the
author, and all incidents are pure invention.

® are Trademarks registered in the United States Patent and
Trademark Office and in other countries.

Printed in U.S.A.

BARBARY WHARF

For more than one hundred years, London's Fleet Street has been the heartbeat of Britain's major newspaper and magazine industries. But decaying buildings and the high cost of inner-city real estate have forced many companies to relocate dockside, down by the Thames River.

The owner of one such company, Sir George Tyrrell, had a dream, a vision of leading his newspaper, the *Sentinel*, into the twenty-first century with a huge, ultramodern complex called Barbary Wharf. But without additional money and time, the dream—and perhaps even the newspaper—will die.

Enter Nick Caspian, international media tycoon. The man with all the desire and the money to take over the *Sentinel*. Now, as joint owners of the paper, Nick Caspian and Gina Tyrrell, Sir George's heir, are often at odds. Their struggle finally comes to a head when a Japanese investor decides *he* wants the *Sentinel*. Will this bring Nick and Gina together? Or will it take an even greater threat—a violent and deadly one—to unite this couple?

Against this backdrop of conspiracy and intrigue, the future of two people who have shared a turbulent journey and the future of the *Sentinel*, the paper that brought them together, unfolds.

BARBARY WHARF

CAST OF CHARACTERS

Gina Tyrrell—The young widow of Sir George Tyrrell's beloved grandson. Devastated by her husband's death, she devoted herself entirely to Sir George's well-being. And now she will devote herself entirely to his paper, the *Sentinel*.

Nick Caspian—International media tycoon with playboy reputation. Owns and operates newspapers all over Europe, and has now set his sights on Britain. Whatever Nick Caspian wants, he usually gets ... and right now he wants the *Sentinel and* Gina Tyrrell ... possibly in that order.

Sir Dermot Gaskell—A senior director of the *Sentinel*. Determined to overthrow Nick Caspian, he has persuaded Gina Tyrrell to back him in a boardroom coup against Nick. Now Sir Dermot awaits the right opportunity to strike.

Colette Tse—Ambitious and extremely attractive feature writer. She is determined to get to the top of her profession and will use any means at her disposal, including her friendship with Nick Caspian, who seems particularly taken with her charms.

Alessa Caspian—Nick Caspian's independent and unconventional sister. She strikes up an immediate friendship with Gina Tyrrell and begins to confide in her all she knows about her irrepressible brother, much to Gina's curiosity and distress.

Mr. Tamaki—One of Japan's, and indeed the world's, wealthiest tycoons. Adamant that his daughter Suki will realize her ambition to run a major newspaper, he has decided to take control of the *Sentinel*—if not buy it outright. If that means the removal of Nick Caspian, so be it!

CHAPTER ONE

JANUARY was a grey month, thought Gina Tyrrell, standing by the boardroom window watching a north wind whipping the surface of the river and making barges rock at their moorings. This year, January was worse than usual: a month which prowled dangerously around the city like a wolf, fanged and watchful.

Behind her she could hear Hazel van Leyden softly talking to Sophie, the girl who was to replace her as Nick Caspian's secretary-in-chief. 'He likes to have a jug of iced water and a glass on this side, a range of pens, pencils, highlighters up here, and the note-pad here and...'

Gina sighed, hating the idea that Hazel would be leaving in a matter of days. They had worked together smoothly for a long time and Gina was going to miss her. It was not a happy start to the year.

But then everything was so dismal; no leaves on the trees, no flowers, no colour anywhere, no sun. Depressing. She had been feeling depressed ever since Christmas. The weather, probably. She couldn't remember a colder winter. In more ways than one.

It had been snowing on and off for weeks; ponds and lakes were frozen, the sky was lightless, birds fell dead from leafless trees, people hurried, heads bent, through the windswept streets—and in Barbary Wharf, in spite of the central heating and double glazing, Gina constantly found herself swinging between chills which made her hands and feet cold and a feverish irritability.

Hazel had noticed her odd moods and as a very old friend had risked asking outright, 'Gina, you're being very weird lately. What *is* wrong with you?'

'I'm sick of this winter weather,' Gina had said, knowing it wasn't that simple.

Hazel had known, too, and given her a dry sideways smile. 'Well, aren't we all? I'm having to watch every step I take. The pavements are absolute death-traps and people are so desperate to get out of the cold that they rush round corners without looking where they're going.'

Gina had immediately forgotten her own problems, looking at her friend with anxious green eyes. 'You're right. Maybe you should stop work at once? If anything went wrong now I'd never forgive myself!'

'Only another couple of weeks—I'm being very careful, don't worry,' Hazel had reassured. In the last month, she was looking far more pregnant, her slim, active body weighed down with the baby she carried. She moved slowly, a little clumsily, often putting a hand to her back in that characteristic gesture of late pregnancy. Looking at her sometimes, Gina barely recognised her. Hazel had changed radically; not merely her body, but her mind. She would be working right next to Gina, but her thoughts kept going off to Holland, where her husband, Piet van Leyden, was already beginning the process of launching their own firm.

His sudden desertion had been a shock for Nick Caspian. Piet had worked as the Caspian International architect, designing new buildings, renovating old ones, ever since Nick took over his father's firm. Nick confided in Piet more than in anyone else who worked for him. He trusted Piet never to repeat a confidence, and would listen to his advice seriously, because they had known each other since they were students; it was a personal relationship rather than a mere business one, and Gina sensed it had hurt Nick when Piet told him he was leaving.

The atmosphere around him had been below zero ever since. It hadn't helped when she had refused to go to San Francisco to spend Christmas with him and his mother. He had flown off in an icy silence and come back a week ago, in much the same mood, after an absence more prolonged than anyone had expected. After San Francisco he had, it seemed, gone on to visit several of his other newspapers, Milan first, and then Berlin, where he was having some local problems with the distribution system.

He had been away nearly three weeks, which was the longest time he had been out of London since he first made a bid to buy the newspaper. Over the past year, the *Sentinel* had absorbed a good deal of his attention, although he frequently visited other parts of his international empire for short periods. When he had to do so, his habit was to leave London on a Sunday evening, spend several days in whichever country demanded his attention, or else fly to Luxembourg, his corporate base, and return mid-week to London.

The telephone in the boardroom rang, making Gina start. Hazel said to Sophie, 'Get that, will you?' and then gave Gina a grimace.

'That will be the first of them. Ten to one it's Henry Harrington—he's usually the first to arrive.'

'Yes, please show Mr Harrington up,' Sophie was saying in her cool, carefully modulated voice on the other side of the panelled room.

Hazel lowered her own voice to a whisper. 'Every inch of her the perfect secretary! She'll do a better job than I ever did.'

'Don't be silly, and don't fish for compliments! Sophie is going to be very efficient and she's a nice girl, but I'll still miss you. You know very well you're irreplaceable as far as I'm concerned.'

Hazel smiled a little mistily. 'Thanks for the ego boost.' She looked at her watch and became instantly brisk. 'We'd better let Nick know they've started arriving.'

'I'll do that,' said Gina, hurrying off. She found Nick at his desk, in his shirt-sleeves, a lean, hard-bitten man with black hair and a strong, chiselled face. He was lounging back in his swivel chair, his highly polished black shoes on the desk, rapidly skim-reading the files on the various subjects which would be discussed at the board meeting.

'Henry's here!' Gina breathlessly told him.

His black lashes lifted to show her his eyes; cold as the north wind and grey as the January sky. She hated it when he looked at her like that. They had been in a state of confrontation all last year, but it hadn't been this icy or hostile. Was Nick still so angry because she wouldn't go to San Francisco with him?

'Then get him a drink and keep him happy until I get there!' His voice was clipped and curt, an order delivered as if she was one of his junior secretaries. Gina bristled with resentment.

'I'm sure Hazel will do that, but I thought you would want to know——'

'Well, now I do, but I'm busy,' he bit out, then a sneer curled his lip. 'Go back and be charming to him; you're good at that.' His eyes went back to the file he was reading, the gesture dismissing her without a word. She took a deep breath, almost losing her temper, then thought better of it.

Wordlessly turning on her heel, she went out, slamming the door behind her so that the sound echoed up and down the whole floor. She could imagine the looks being exchanged by everyone else who worked within earshot. She knew how people gossiped at Barbary Wharf; gossip was the breath of life to them, especially if it concerned the two people who between them owned a majority of shares in the *Sentinel*. Now that they had heard her slam that door, speculation would be rife.

As she walked back towards the boardroom, she almost collided with the features editor of the newspaper, Colette Tse, coming out of the lift. Colette gave her a smile, did a double-take as she noticed Gina's expression, and raised her perfectly pencilled eyebrows.

'Trouble?'

'He always is!' Gina indiscreetly muttered, and Colette gave one of her feline little smiles, her almond-shaped black eyes amused.

'Nick? Yes, he is being difficult lately, but men always hate having their routine upset—and at the moment his life has been turned upside-down with Piet and Hazel both walking out on him at the same time. Take my advice, soothe him down when he gets into one of his moods—don't argue with him!'

Gina bristled, her face angrily flushed. What did Colette know about Nick's moods? She knew what she could do with her advice!

She didn't bother to reply, just made a big show of looking at her watch. 'I have to get to the boardroom, or I'll be late.'

She rushed off but couldn't stop speculating about what was going on in Colette's mind. She had never understood Colette. A strong-minded, beautiful woman with a Chinese father and an English mother, Colette was in her thirties. She hadn't married and at the moment was between men, but she had been very successful professionally. Not as successful as Colette herself wished, though. The career prizes in journalism weren't glittering enough for her. It was as clear as crystal that she was determined to climb to the top in the Caspian organisation. Every time a higher executive position came up, Colette applied for it.

She made no secret of the fact that she wanted to get out of journalism and into the world of the newspaper executive, with a high salary, lots of travel all expenses paid, a glossy car and great clothes.

Gina had never been sure whether or not she liked her. She certainly respected her professional expertise and admired her clothes sense and the stylish looks which made her one of the most striking women working in the building. But there was a toughness, even a hardness, in Colette which grated on Gina. She was very much a man's woman, and no doubt she would achieve all her ambitions in time; Nick obviously had his eyes on her. He always advanced talent, but Colette had more than that to recommend her. Her looks would have attracted his attention at once, and, from the way she had been talking a moment ago, Nick had caught Colette's eye, too. Gina had picked up a very personal note in Colette's voice when she talked about him.

It hadn't been her imagination, Gina was sure of that. A little frown knitted her brows as she opened the boardroom door. Colette was ambitious and Nick would be the biggest catch any woman could dream of making—had she got her sights set on him?

'Ah, here she is!' Hazel's voice said in relief, and Gina pulled herself together, smiling warmly as she went to meet Henry Harrington.

'Gina, my dear,' he said, taking both her hands and gazing at her fondly before leaning over to kiss her cheek.

He was a large man in his sixties with iron-grey hair and a fresh complexion, a fatherly manner and very little interest in anything but golf, which he played with the obsessive fervour of the religious convert. He had been appointed to the board of directors by Sir George Tyrrell, the previous proprietor of the *Sentinel*, a close friend of his. Gina had known Henry ever since she'd married James Tyrrell, Sir George's grandson, but she had only really become fond of him when her husband was killed.

Both she and Sir George had been devastated by that loss, and Henry Harrington had come along to the house and forced them out on drives into the country; he had come to dinner and made Sir George play cards or back-gammon with him; he had taken them to the theatre. They had both been so bleakly unhappy that left to their own devices they would have sunk into despair, but Henry had not let them do so. He had been there, dragging them out, in spite of their reluctance and irritable protests. They had not wanted his help, they had not been grateful then, but, looking back, Gina was grateful. He had saved her sanity.

'I'm the first, again,' Henry said, beaming.

'You always are, Henry!'

He chuckled. 'First here, first to leave, that's my motto! Do my duty and vanish!'

'Off to the golf course!' Gina teased and he grinned.

'Only wish I could! Can't play in this weather—the greens are ankle-deep in snow, damn it!'

Henry was a very rich man, who had spent most of his life running his family company, manufacturing machinery. He had retired now, leaving the firm to be run by his eldest son, Johnny, who had ten times his father's energy and was already proving himself a powerhouse. Henry had happily handed over the reins as soon as Johnny had shown signs of wanting them, and retired to do what he really enjoyed, play golf all day, but he had several directorships which gave him a good income as well as the income he had from his own company. Henry was the sort of director many companies liked: he turned up regularly, was always amiable, voted as required, and didn't interfere in business. No wonder Nick Caspian was happy to keep him on the board!

'How's your handicap now?' asked Gina indulgently, watching him sip his whisky. He had been ordered to cut right down on spirits after a slight stroke last summer, but still had one drink before every board meeting. He claimed it was medicinal and helped him get through a boring day.

Henry was only too eager to talk about his golf and was still talking about it when several other directors arrived.

Over the past year a number of directors had left the board, one from ill health, one having died, others resigning over clashes with Nick; and Nick had replaced them all by men he chose. Admittedly, there had been discussions on the subject, and the board had voted on Nick's choices, but nobody had seriously opposed him or put up anyone else in preference, except Gina.

She had several times put up a fight, but it had never been a determined one, largely because it had taken her all this time to find her feet and become confident enough to challenge Nick to a real battle.

Their confrontations had all been minor ones so far, but she was becoming more sure of herself with each day that passed, and she had begun to develop a political sense; to assess the other directors, speculating on whether they would be hostile, neutral or likely to support a move against Nick.

Late last year, one of the board, another old friend of Sir George Tyrrell, Sir Dermot Gaskell, had approached her to ask if she would join a group planning to outmanoeuvre Nick Caspian on the board by outvoting him on major issues, with the hope of forcing him to resign. If Nick lost the confidence of a majority of the board of directors his position on the *Sentinel* would be seriously weakened, but any attack on him would have to be backed up by a major shareholder.

When Sir George Tyrrell had died of a heart attack on discovering that Nick was making secret moves to gain complete control of the newspaper, Gina had been so distressed and bitter that she had sworn to make Nick pay for it, but the passing of time had watered down her hostility. She had had too much to think about, too much had happened since, not least that she had seen Nick almost every day, and now knew him far better than she had a year ago. It was very difficult to sustain hatred of someone you knew as well as she now knew Nick.

Sir Dermot's plot had, therefore, disturbed her. She simply hadn't been sure what she wanted to do. Oh, she still told herself she wanted to avenge Sir George, but, faced with the chance to do just that, she had hesitated, her mind confused.

Sir Dermot had angrily reproached her; reminded her how much she owed to her dead husband and his family, and pointed out that, as she was the only other major shareholder, it was essential to his plan for her to be one of the conspiracy against Nick.

She had had no choice. How could she refuse to join Nick's enemies when she had sworn, publicly, that one day she would force him to give up control of the *Sentinel*?

Sir Dermot had been very relieved. He told her she could leave the arrangements to him, he would talk to her again when he had put together a strong group to support them on the board. Had he done so? she wondered, looking around the room.

Gina had seen Sir Dermot, at the engagement party of another of the directors, Philip Slade, but Nick had been there, too, which had made it impossible to say anything she hadn't wanted Nick to hear.

She didn't even know when Sir Dermot meant to launch his attack and was nervously hoping it wouldn't be too soon. She was dreading it. The thought of Nick's expression when he realised what was going on made her skin creep, so she had tried to forget all about Sir Dermot's plans over Christmas.

She had spent the holiday with the foreign editor, Daniel Bruneille, and the girl he lived with, Roz Amery, an old schoolfriend of Gina's. It had been a family Christmas because Roz's father and half-sister, Irena, had joined them, along with Irena's husband, Esteban, a marketing director, who also worked for Caspian

International. It had been a relaxed and casual holiday,
but somehow Gina kept remembering Nick's face when
she refused to spend Christmas with him and his mother,
and wincing at the memory.

Hazel sidled up to her at that instant. 'Where's Nick?'

'Coming in his own sweet time,' Gina muttered, pale
and frowning.

'Oh,' said Hazel, eyeing her shrewdly. 'Like that, is
it?'

Gina glared. 'Don't tell me you haven't noticed how
impossible he is lately!'

'Of course I have! He's been like a bear with a sore
head ever since Piet resigned,' lamented Hazel, sitting
down on the nearest chair with a sigh of exhaustion.
'He'll never forgive us, you know. He takes it personally, and he won't see it from our point of view. It's
very upsetting for Piet; all those years of slaving away
for Nick, and now that he wants to do something of his
own Nick's treating him as if he had stabbed him in the
back, and he's being very offhand with me, too.'

'He's self-obsessed—sees everything from his own side
of the question, and other people aren't supposed to have
a viewpoint.' Gina looked at Hazel closely. 'Are you OK?
You're very pale.'

'It's standing up for ages—it gives me backache and
makes me feel sick!'

'Then go and lie down!' Gina protested, anxiously
studying her friend.

'I'm going to sit down all through the meeting, don't
worry.' Hazel's eyes wandered around the room, and she
mentally ticked people off her list of directors. 'I think
they're all here. Maybe we should give Nick a buzz to
hurry him up?'

Gina looked around, too, frowning. 'No, Sir Dermot
hasn't arrived yet and neither has Philip.'

'There's Philip, walking in now,' Hazel told her, and
lowered her voice. 'I forgot to ask...you went to his

engagement party, didn't you? What's his Japanese fiancée like?'

Gina thought back to the engagement party and the girl Philip had proudly introduced to her. 'Very beautiful,' she said. 'Her name's Suki Tamaki. She's incredibly fine-boned and slender, I don't suppose she's ever had a dieting problem in her life, and she has this wonderful complexion. But she's more American than Japanese, in the way she talks, what she wears. Her evening dress had "made in Paris" stamped all over it, actually, but she bought it in Los Angeles, she said. She was born in California, she told me; she's never lived anywhere else.'

'Did her family come over to London with her?'

Gina nodded. 'They were there. Her mother never said a word, she just smiled and bowed to everyone and followed her husband around everywhere; she had a big white chrysanthemum in her hair, a real one, and she wore a pink and white kimono with the most enormous pink sash! Mr Tamaki just wore a suit, and he talked for both of them—he spoke very good English...'

'American accent, though?' suggested Hazel and Gina nodded.

'Of course...' Her voice died away as she saw Philip Slade heading towards them. A slim, tanned, boyish young man with floppy brown hair and blue eyes, he missed good looks somehow, perhaps because of a weakness about his mouth. There was nothing impressive about Philip, but he had a very appealing smile.

'Hello, Gina, dear,' he said, kissing her cheek. 'You look as fabulous as usual.'

'Thank you, Philip, so do you,' she said, amused. 'How's Suki? Is she still in London, or has she gone back to the States?'

'Her parents went back last week, but Suki's still here, staying with my aunt Regina. They're having a wonderful time planning our wedding.' His eyes sparkled triumphantly. 'There was a bit of trouble over it, but Suki got her own way, she always does . . .' His grin was admiring; clearly Philip delighted in his future wife's will-power. 'She wanted it in London; she feels it will be chic. She's got Aunt Regina to ring all her friends, pull out all the stops, to make it the wedding of the year. At the moment, they're talking about St Margaret's, Westminster Abbey, and Aunt Regina's son, Basil, is in the House of Commons, so we might even have our reception on the terrace there.'

Hazel's face was a picture. 'Won't that be a thrill?' she said drily, meeting Gina's eyes and silently conveying her real feelings.

Gina had difficulty not laughing.

Philip didn't pick up the sarcasm. 'Well, I can stand it if it makes Suki happy,' he said. 'But I'm glad to get away for a few hours. I can't understand why women love talking about weddings.' His blue eyes travelled down over Gina's slender figure, almost absently, then, as if realising he was staring, he said, 'I like the dress, Gina. It suits you.'

'Thank you, Philip,' she smiled. She hadn't been too sure about the vivid green knitted wool dress with a polo neck and long sleeves—very warm, it was perfect for this cold weather, but Gina had suspected that the green shade was a little too vibrant. She was always trying to tone down her russet hair with the right colours; give herself a classy look, like Sophie Watson, who always seemed so elegant. It never quite seemed to come off, though! Something in her own nature matched her bright hair and made it impossible for her to look as cool and assured as Sophie.

'Sir Dermot not here yet?' asked Philip, glancing around for him, and Gina shook her head.

Hazel got up. 'I'll ring Nick.'

'It'll do it—you sit down,' Gina said, walking over to the phone on the wall near the window.

She dialled Nick's private number in the office and his voice snapped, 'Yes?'

'Everyone is here, and waiting,' Gina said as shortly, not bothering to add that Sir Dermot wasn't yet here.

She glanced down out of the window and saw him at that second, his grey hair blowing in the wind, his body hunched inside his camel-hair overcoat, getting out of his Rolls-Royce just outside the main entrance.

'I'll be there in a moment!' Nick bit out, hanging up.

Gina put down her own phone, feeling like swearing or screaming or kicking the wall. How much longer was he going to keep this up?

She was so angry that she couldn't turn and face the others in the room for a moment and stood with her back to them, staring out of the window and absently watching Sir Dermot, who was hurrying along the snow-covered walkway towards the entrance. Suddenly the old man skidded on a patch of ice on the path. She saw him lurch out of control; his arms flew up; his briefcase sailed out of his hand, and Sir Dermot pitched backwards and fell down.

Gina gave a shocked cry. Everyone in the boardroom turned to stare. Outside, Sir Dermot lay still for a moment, then tried to struggle up, on his elbows, only to fall back again. From this height, through double glazing, it was impossible to hear anything, but Gina could have sworn he had given a cry of pain.

'What is it?' asked Philip, joining her to stare down.

'Sir Dermot has had an accident!' She picked up the phone again and dialled the head porter's number downstairs in the reception area.

'Head porter's desk . . .' his stately voice told her.

'This is Mrs Tyrrell. I just saw Sir Dermot Gaskell fall over on the walkway outside the main entrance.'

The head porter sounded startled. 'I'll go straight out and have a look, Mrs Tyrrell . . .'

'Yes, do that, but don't move him yet, I'm coming down myself, after I've rung the doctor on call. Sir Dermot shouldn't be moved until the doctor has seen him.'

She rang off, then dialled the doctor who was always on call, with a qualified nurse, in the medical suite on the ground floor of the building. Once he had been alerted Gina turned to leave, pushing through the little crowd of directors craning to stare down at Sir Dermot.

'I'll come with you,' said Philip, his face set in a frown. His concern for Sir Dermot surprised her a little. They had never seemed to be that close, but of course Sir Dermot had been wooing him lately, intent on getting him to co-operate in the planned take-over of the board.

Henry Harrington tried to buttonhole her as she left. 'I'm not surprised, you know. That snow should have been cleared away first thing this morning! When I arrived I almost slipped over. I said to the porter on the door that somebody ought to clear the paths but of course they take no notice.'

'I'm sorry, Henry, I can't stop,' she said, hurrying away. He was quite right, of course: the snow should have been shovelled off the paths; it should be done each morning while the snow lasted. She would have to get the works manager to issue an order to that effect at once. She couldn't imagine why it had not been done automatically.

'I wonder if the company is liable—after all, snow is an act of God,' she heard one of the other directors say just before she left the room.

Gina gave Philip a wry look. 'Typical! They're already looking for ways of getting out of any responsibility for Sir Dermot's accident.'

He grimaced. 'Well, it could be a very expensive accident for the *Sentinel* if Sir Dermot is badly injured.'

They both collected their coats because it was much too cold to go outside without them, then headed for the lift, only to walk straight into Nick, who scowled at them in narrow-eyed surprise. 'Where are you going?'

She told him what she had seen from the window. 'I've rung the doctor, but I'm going down there now to see what damage he did himself. From the way he fell I'm afraid it might be serious.'

Nick's brows met. 'I'd better come down with you.' He gave Philip an unsmiling stare. 'Would you go back to the boardroom and apologise for this delay, Slade? Ask them to wait. I shouldn't be more than ten minutes. Get Hazel and Sophie to organise coffee, or another drink for those who prefer that.'

Philip didn't have time to argue; the lift doors closed on his furious face. Gina didn't look at Nick. A thick silence surrounded them. She had no real idea what he was thinking, but she knew he was still in a temper. Nothing new in that. He had been angry ever since Christmas. The air vibrated with his anger whenever she saw him. Gina hated it, she felt sick every time she met his eyes and saw the black ice of his rage in them, but slowly she was getting angry too. He had no right to speak to her, look at her, like that.

If anyone had behaved badly it was him, not her, but he expected her to forget everything that had happened in the past: the way he had betrayed her, his treachery to Sir George, the old man's death. Nick could not see that he had behaved badly; to him it was just business. He had wanted control of the *Sentinel*, been prepared to do anything necessary to get it. He had been ready to seduce her, even marry her, but when an easier path had presented itself, and he'd thought he could buy a controlling interest without needing to marry her, he had jumped at the chance. It all seemed very reasonable to Nick. He could not see why she was so angry; he thought she was being childish in resenting what he had done.

When they reached the ground floor he strode out across the foyer and Gina almost had to run to keep up with him, but Nick didn't slow his pace because of that. He seemed totally unaware of her hurrying along beside him, but Gina knew better. Nick was deliberately making her run to keep up. She threw him a furious look; his profile was inimical, rigid.

They found a little crowd gathered around Sir Dermot; Nick pushed his way through them, frowning.

'Get back to work, all of you—what do you think this is? Street theatre?'

They hurriedly vanished without a word, except for the head porter who saluted Nick, a hand smartly touching his gold-braided cap. 'I did what I could for the old gentleman until the doctor came, sir. He seemed in a lot of pain, I'm afraid. It doesn't look too good.'

Nick nodded curtly. 'Has someone sent for an ambulance? He ought to go to hospital.'

'The doctor rang them, sir.'

The company doctor, a young man in his late twenties, who had done several years in a general hospital before joining the *Sentinel*, was kneeling beside Sir Dermot, his body blocking Gina's view of the old man's face. He had freed one of Sir Dermot's arms from his thick overcoat and jacket, had rolled up the blue and white striped shirt-sleeve, and was giving him an injection in his bared arm.

Gina winced, looking away. She hated the very sight of hypodermic needles.

'What's the situation, Dr Massingham?' Nick asked, and the doctor glanced around.

'Mr Caspian?' He sounded incredulous. 'Er—good morning,' he stammered, face flushed and startled as he got to his feet. Before he answered Nick's question he moved slightly away from Sir Dermot and spoke in lowered tones. 'A broken leg, I'm afraid. He's lucky he didn't break his hip with a fall like that—he might just as easily have done so. I've given him a shot to help the pain, which is considerable, poor chap. He'll have to go to hospital to have the leg X-rayed and put in plaster, and it might be wise for him to stay there for a day or two, for observation. This sort of shock can have serious after-effects with a man of his age. I've already rung for an ambulance, and I'll go with him.'

'Can't we take him inside? It's freezing out here,' Gina said anxiously, kneeling down beside Sir Dermot. He had his eyes closed, beads of sweat stood out on his pale face, in spite of the cold, and she could hear his teeth chattering.

'That wouldn't be wise, in view of the broken leg,' said Dr Massingham, his dark eyes grave. 'The less he moves the better until he has been X-rayed. I can't be sure he hasn't suffered some internal injury until I see the results.'

The wail of an ambulance was heard at that moment, and Nick and the doctor walked towards the main gate. Sir Dermot opened his eyes and looked up at Gina, his lips moving soundlessly.

She took one of his hands in hers and smiled. 'You're going to be OK, Dermot, don't worry, it isn't anything serious,' she soothed.

'Slade...' he whispered.

'Philip?' Gina frowned.

'Tell Slade...' He broke off, shivering, and Gina looked at him anxiously. He looked years older suddenly.

'Forget about business, Dermot, you just take care of yourself!'

'Listen...there isn't much time, Gina,' Sir Dermot muttered fretfully. 'Tell him to wait.' He gripped her hand, staring urgently at her. 'Got that? Tell him...wait.'

'Wait?' she repeated, frowning. There was an almost feverish anxiety in Sir Dermot's eyes, and Gina was troubled. 'Wait for what?'

He made a weak, irritable gesture. 'Slade will understand. Tell him it will have to be shelved until I'm well again. He must be patient.'

The ambulance men arrived while he was still talking. 'Stand back, please, miss,' one of them said.

Gina stepped back. They carefully moved Sir Dermot on to their stretcher and five minutes later drove off with him and Dr Massingham.

She looked round to find Nick watching her, his eyes sharp. 'What was he talking about?'

She shrugged. 'He was rambling, not making much sense. Whatever the doctor gave him made him light-headed.' But she suspected she knew what Sir Dermot had meant.

'I wonder,' said Nick slowly. 'Sir Dermot and Philip Slade...now what do they have in common? And what is Slade going to have to be patient about?'

Gina felt his hard, searching eyes on her, and nervously chattered at him, 'Who knows? He didn't explain. Maybe they play golf together? I sometimes think we should have board meetings on the golf course; we'd get a much better turn-out than we usually do.' She looked at her watch. 'Talking about board meetings...hadn't we better get back there? We're already forty minutes late.'

Nick didn't pursue the matter. He followed her up to the boardroom without mentioning Sir Dermot again, but Gina was not fooled into a false sense of security. Nick's mind was as sharp as a razor. What if he guessed that Sir Dermot and Philip were plotting against him? Gina turned icy cold from head to foot as she contemplated how he would react to that!

CHAPTER TWO

THE arctic conditions seemed to drag on forever, but in fact it was only a week before the temperature rose overnight, the wind changed quarters and there was a thaw. Everyone had to go on wearing boots whenever they went out, but now they were wading through dirty grey slush which squelched and oozed under their feet, and the gutters gurgled, filled to overflowing with melting snow.

Gina visited Sir Dermot that weekend, at the private clinic near St Albans, where he was convalescing in the Hertfordshire countryside, taking him a basket of carefully chosen tropical fruit from Harrods, and a new book on golf strategy.

When she tapped on the door and peeped in she found him sitting in a chair by the window, wearing dark red silk pyjamas and a black and red striped dressing-gown. Looking round, he gave her a wicked grin. 'Come in, Red Riding Hood, and give Grandma a big kiss.'

She laughed, coming over to kiss his cheek. 'I'm glad to see you're recovering fast!' He was a much better colour than he had been last time she saw him, his eyes brighter, more alert.

'I'm getting bored, anyway,' he grimaced. 'They tell me that's a sign of recovery! Would you like some tea? They bring some at three o'clock—I hear them coming along now.'

Gina had passed the trolley rattling along the corridor. She looked doubtful. 'Are visitors allowed to...?'

'Of course they are! It all goes on my bill. The more the merrier, that's their motto.' Sir Dermot smiled at her. 'I can't tell you how pleased I am to see you, Gina;

it's very good of you to come all this way.' He gestured to another chair. 'Pull that over here, sit down and tell me all the news—how's the *Sentinel* going on? Anything exciting happen since my accident?'

'Not that I can think of!' She handed him the book she had brought. 'I hope you haven't got this!'

'No, I haven't, Gina, but by a strange coincidence I've just read a rave review of it. You are brilliant!' He riffled the pages, smiling.

Gina took the basket of fruit over to his bedside table; he had several vases of flowers, and she was glad she hadn't brought any. There was a silver basket of red hot-house roses, too; a card dangling from the red ribbon around the basket. Gina bent to smell the flowers; they were scentless. She saw Philip Slade's name on the card.

'I had been lying here wishing I was out on the golf course, but now I can improve my game without actually needing to play!' Sir Dermot closed the book and put it down as the door opened and the trolley rattled into the room, pushed by a very small nurse in a striped blue and white uniform, her head dwarfed by a large white cap.

'My visitor would like some tea, Nurse,' Sir Dermot told her.

The girl nodded, concentrating on picking up tiny, thin sandwiches with a pair of tongs far too big for them. She managed to transfer two of them to two plates, added a very thin piece of fruit cake each, then poured two cups of tea. 'Milk or lemon?'

'Milk,' said Gina, accepting the cup, which she put down on the floor, and a plate.

The trolley rattled out again. Gina bit into a sandwich: cucumber, she noted.

'I gave Philip your message,' she told Sir Dermot, who turned his face to the window, his body rigid.

'What message?' he asked, but she suspected he knew very well what she was talking about.

'Don't you remember?' she drily asked. 'When you had your accident, before they put you in the ambulance, you said to me: "tell Slade to wait".'

'I did?' Sir Dermot laughed a little too loudly. 'I don't remember that. Obviously I was worrying about the board meeting, about not being able to get there. Not like me to have a conscience about work; I must have been delirious.'

'You haven't heard from Philip?'

Sir Dermot's eyes flicked to the red roses. 'No,' he said. 'We're not that friendly, you know.' He smiled at her warmly. 'Eat your cake, Gina, it's quite good.'

Driving back to London, Gina brooded on the lie and wondered why Sir Dermot should lie to her. He had told her he was planning some sort of attack on Nick, he had asked her to back him—so why should he be reluctant to admit Philip was involved? Come to that, why was Philip so cagey?

When she gave him Sir Dermot's odd message, Philip had distinctly looked taken aback, had reddened. 'Wait . . . ?' he had stammered, obviously unnerved by Nick Caspian's watchful eyes, then he had pulled himself together. 'I can't think what he means!' He shot another look at Nick, licked his lips, swallowed, broke out with an air of inspiration, 'Of course . . . we did say we would play a round of golf together; that's what he must have meant.'

At the time she had simply been sorry for him, more preoccupied with Nick's mood than anything else, believing anyway that she understood his uneasiness, but now she looked back and thought: What are the two of them up to, Sir Dermot and Philip? She had been sure she knew but now she was less certain—but one thing was clear enough: they were not going to tell her too much about their plans.

Was that because they didn't trust her? Heat kindled in her face, and her green eyes grew brilliant with anger and distress. Did they think she might warn Nick? Might betray them to him?

Without her realising it, her foot pressed down on the accelerator, and she stared blankly ahead, not even seeing what was in front of her, a prey to anguish and shame. It was lucky there was not much traffic going back into London that Saturday afternoon. Gina roared past slower moving cars without noticing them, her teeth biting down into her lower lip, her green eyes wide and frozen.

If they felt they couldn't trust her, that had to mean that they knew...well, guessed at least...how deep her feelings for Nick were!

She flinched, hating that thought. She had struggled with her love for Nick for a year, seeing him day after day, forcing her feelings down out of sight, suffocating them with all the reasons why she couldn't love him, why she had to hate him—and the possibility of other people watching, guessing, reading her secret, was unbearable.

She spent that Sunday with Hazel, helping her pack up all of her possessions, ready for the move to Holland. Piet was flying in on Tuesday, for Hazel's farewell party, and the removal people would come two days later. By the end of the week Hazel would be established in her new home, in Middelburg.

'You must come and stay,' she said, neatly packing linen. 'You don't know Holland, do you? I'm sure you'll like it—do come, Gina. I already feel at home there; going backwards and forwards all these months I've had time to get used to life there. Of course, in lots of ways it's very similar to England, and now I'm learning Dutch I'm finding it surprisingly easy because so many words sound the same as ours...I mean, if you say *biefstuck* you get steak...or *appeltaart*...well, that's obvious. You could get by just speaking English, but I want to be able to talk to Piet in his own language, and I want our children to be bilingual.'

Gina was wrapping china in newspaper, carefully placing it in another packing case, with lots of protective padding between the pieces.

'The first thing you must do when you get there is find a doctor and get yourself booked into a hospital for the birth.'

'Piet has dealt with all that. He's very efficient, you know!' Hazel gave her a smile brimming with pride. 'And at the moment he's so full of enthusiasm, he's racing around working like a demon. I hadn't realised quite how badly he wanted to set up on his own. He's so happy, you wouldn't believe it!'

'I'm glad. I'm really looking forward to seeing him again and hearing all his news.'

Hazel's smile faded a little and she sighed. 'I only wish Nick wasn't being such a pain!'

Gina stopped smiling, too. 'Yes.'

'Considering the years Piet has worked for him, you'd think Nick could be a little more gracious, wouldn't you? Can't he understand why Piet wants to have his own company, be his own boss now? I think getting married, becoming a family man, made Piet realise it was time he left Nick and branched out on his own—he wants to build a future for our children.'

'And that's very natural—in his place Nick would feel exactly the same!' soothed Gina, and Hazel lifted a flushed, resentful face to her.

'Of course he would! But that would be different! Nick is entitled to anything he can get, but if one of his serfs tries to escape . . . watch out!'

Gina laughed, but Hazel was too angry to find it funny.

'I'm serious! That's how he sees us, anyone who works for him. As one of his possessions. Piet's a runaway slave, in Nick's book. Any day now I expect him to set the bloodhounds on our trail, turn up, whip in hand, and threaten to clap us both in irons!' She broke off with a heavy sigh. 'And it is upsetting Piet. They've been friends for so long, he really feels Nick's hostility.' She looked pleadingly at Gina. 'Can't you talk to him, Gina? Tell him he isn't being fair, get him to stop treating Piet as if he was suddenly an enemy?'

Gina hesitated, making a face. 'At the moment, he's hardly speaking to me, either! If he does, he bites my head off, and if he doesn't he glowers at me as if he *wants* to bite my head off!' Hazel's unhappy face went on pleading, and Gina looked into it, and sighed. 'Oh, OK, I'll try.'

'Oh, thank you...' Hazel breathed, hugging her, with some difficulty because of her present bulk.

Gina began to giggle. 'These days a hug from you is like a hug from a hippopotamus!'

That made Hazel laugh and from then on she was much happier, but Gina was nervous, contemplating her next encounter with Nick. She was under no illusions. It was not going to be easy to get him to listen; he was more likely to turn on her and make her wish she had never raised the subject.

Next morning, over a light breakfast of grapefruit, bran flakes and orange juice, she read the first edition of the *Sentinel* which was always delivered to her door in the early hours of the morning, when copies were brought to Nick, too, by special messenger.

The front page was dominated by a political scandal that morning, but Gina was more interested in Tom Birny's continuing story about the East End of London gang families.

The first series of articles had caused an enormous storm last month; there had been angry threats of lawsuits from members of the families and even several threats against Tom Birny's life, but all that seemed to have died down over Christmas. Gina read her way carefully through the new article, looked at the photos published alongside it, and grimaced, hoping that Tom knew what he was doing. Had the legal department really passed this as safe for publication? What was Guy Faulkner thinking about? Even if every word in the article was true, it wouldn't be easy to prove, especially as the police seemed unable to nail these men. According to Tom they always had alibis whenever a major crime was committed, so how could the *Sentinel* risk publishing unsubstantiated allegations like this? If any of these men decided to sue, they could win enormous damages. If they all did, the *Sentinel* would be in serious financial trouble.

Gina left for work, gripping her copy of the paper under her arm, her face flushed and angry. She was about to get into her car in the car park when she saw Nick striding towards his own vehicle.

Gina moved into his path, holding out her newspaper. 'Have you seen Tom Birny's latest piece?'

'Yes,' Nick bit out, glowering. He moved to walk past and she blocked him again.

'Did you know it was going in?'

'Yes!' He looked at her with a scowl. 'Look, I'm in a hurry——'

She didn't get out of his way. 'You knew?' Gina was incredulous. 'But did you actually read it first?'

'You know the new ruling that I have to give my OK to anything which could be sensitive!' he muttered, his black brows lowered. 'Of course I read Birny's article.'

'And you let it go ahead?'

Nick's grey eyes flashed. 'Are you questioning my authority or my professional ability, Gina? Do I really have to remind you that I've been running newspapers since I was a very young man? I read the article, I knew the risks, and on balance I decided to go ahead and publish. I believe Birny is performing a public service in letting the whole country know exactly what these people are up to, and I'm damned if I'll apologise to you for my decision.'

Before she could recover from the charged rage in his voice he had walked past, got into his white Ferrari and roared out of the car park, leaving Gina still trembling from the encounter.

It was only as she walked into her office, in Barbary Wharf, later, and saw Hazel's hopeful, questioning eyes, that she realised the brief incident had probably made it even harder for her to talk to him about Piet and Hazel; he was going to be even angrier with her now. She and Nick seemed destined to be enemies.

'Sorry, Hazel,' she muttered. 'I haven't had a chance to talk to him yet. I'll try later. Has he got any free time?'

Hazel shook her head gloomily. 'His diary is crammed with appointments all day. He's got Colette Tse in there at the moment——'

'Colette?' Gina asked sharply, stiffening.

Hazel looked at her in surprise. 'Yes. The features editor, you know.'

'I know,' said Gina. 'Did Nick send for her, or...?'

'She rang, yesterday, talked to Nick for a minute then he put her back to me and told me to give her an appointment for this morning. Why?' Hazel was looking curious, and Gina glanced away, shrugging.

'Oh...I just wondered. It seemed odd.'

There was no earthly reason why Colette Tse shouldn't be closeted with Nick, except, of course, that her job did not normally bring her into direct contact with the proprietor. Whatever she had to say should have been said to the editor of the paper, Fabien Arnaud. Nick had been interfering in editorial contact ever since he took over, however. He was intent on changing the *Sentinel* from a serious, if rather staid newspaper into a bright and popular tabloid. All his changes of staff, his direct interventions in editorial policy, had been directed to that end. Gina was utterly opposed to him; the new *Sentinel* horrified her but she had had very little success in halting the process.

'I did wonder about that myself,' said Hazel drily. 'Maybe she talked to Fabien about some project and he turned it down, so she's trying to get Nick to back her. Colette has the gall for that sort of backstairs politics.'

'Nick shouldn't encourage her, though!' Gina said sharply. 'If that is what she's up to! And I wouldn't be surprised; as you say, she has the gall for it.'

'She's one very tough cookie,' Hazel said and Gina nodded.

'She'll need to be if she's going behind Fabien's back to get one of his decisions overturned. Fabien may have to give in to Nick, but he's going to hate Colette for it.'

Sophie hurried in at that moment, flushed and breathless. 'Sorry I'm late, I had to call in at the legal department to sort out Guy's new secretary. He isn't very pleased with her...'

'After you, why would he be?' teased Hazel, and Sophie blushed.

'No, seriously, she can't spell and he keeps catching her having private chats on the phone... he wanted me to talk to her, warn her he would sack her if she didn't improve.' She sighed. 'Well, I tried, but she was chewing bubblegum and almost laughed in my face! I feel bad about this, because, if I hadn't left, Guy wouldn't be having this problem. Maybe I should go back...'

Hazel looked alarmed. 'Oh, no... you can't... who would take over here?'

Gina quickly said, 'Is she from the secretarial pool? Who chose her? You, or Guy Faulkner?'

'Guy did,' Sophie said wryly, making a face. 'I wasn't too pleased at the time. She's a strawberry blonde with a wonderful figure and an IQ of about six. I never thought she could do the job, but I didn't want Guy to think I was jealous.'

Hazel and Gina laughed.

'Look,' Gina said, 'you go down to the pool now and talk to Mrs Withers, tell her I said you were to pick out someone else. The other girl can go back to the pool, and if she doesn't change her attitude she will have to leave us altogether.'

'Thanks,' Sophie said, glowing, and departed in a hurry. When she had gone Gina leaned over Hazel's desk to look at Nick's diary.

'He must have some free time today!'

'There are five more appointments set up before lunch,' said Hazel flatly. 'He's having that with the Minister for Trade...'

'What about dinner?'

'The Russian Ambassador, at the Russian embassy. A very high society occasion indeed, so I'm told! Tonight, half the British government will be there, not to mention some of the *crème de la crème* of British industry. Caviare and the very best ice-cold vodka!'

'Lucky Nick!' Gina laughed, hoping Hazel couldn't see her relief as she realised she wouldn't have to talk to Nick today.

'Tomorrow, then!' she said.

'My last day! And Piet is coming to my party, remember, so please...please, sort it out by then!' Hazel's mouth turned down at the corners, and Gina felt the sting of guilt.

Whether Nick shouted at her or not, she had to do what she could for Hazel! She owed her that much after years of friendship.

Taking a deep breath, 'I'll have talked to him by the time your party starts!' she promised, and Hazel gave her a tremulous smile.

'You're a darling, thanks.'

During their lunchbreak Gina and Roz went to the Barbary Wharf hotel, which was part of the same complex as the offices and printing works of the *Sentinel*, to make the final arrangements for Hazel's farewell party the following evening. Gina was hosting it: she had made most of the decisions and although Nick had offered to pay for it Gina had insisted on doing so herself, because, she pointed out, Hazel had worked for the Tyrrells far longer than she had for Caspian International.

Nick hadn't liked that. His face had tensed and turned cold, the way it always did these days if she mentioned her dead husband's family. Gina hadn't let that deter her, though. She was determined to make Hazel's party a very special occasion, and she wanted to be responsible for it herself.

It was to be a buffet-supper party, with hot and cold food available, which Gina had asked Hazel to choose from the printed menus supplied by the hotel. She had asked for a hot chicken dish in white wine sauce, with sliced mushrooms and white grapes, and wild rice; chilli beef and rice, a range of prepared salads, cold sliced ham and turkey, and for sweets a choice of fresh fruit salad, cheesecake or trifle. There would be cheese and biscuits for those who wanted that.

Everyone would be greeted with a glass of sherry, there would be red or white wine available on all the tables, and for the toasts which would come at the end of the meal there was to be champagne.

Roz and Gina went through every tiny detail with patient determination. Nothing must go wrong on Hazel's last night.

'This is the final figure? Sure?' the hotel manager asked Gina, as she passed him a sheet of paper on which were typed the names of the invited guests and the number who had definitely accepted. The top management of the *Sentinel* would all be there, including some of the directors; people from every department of the newspaper, and, of course, all of Hazel and Piet's personal friends from Barbary Wharf.

'I hope so,' said Gina.

Roz said softly, 'But it is always possible that we might get a few gatecrashers. Everyone in the firm knows about the party and some people who weren't invited might feel they should have been!'

The manager, Romero Montegna, a slim, olive-skinned Sicilian, gave a thin smile. 'You sent invitation cards? Then nobody without a card will get past my security men.'

Alarmed, Gina said, 'We don't want any trouble. This is meant to be a happy occasion.'

Roz grinned at the hotel manager. 'Look, if someone turns up without a card, ask one of us to identify them before you throw them down the front steps.'

'Unless he claims to be Nick Caspian,' Gina said. 'Just chuck him out as soon as you see him.'

Romero Montegna looked stunned for a second, then gave a bark of laughter. 'Oh, a joke...' he said. 'Ha ha! Don't worry, I will deal with any trouble and not make the scene.'

'Good,' Roz said, watching Gina thoughtfully as she laughed a little too wildly. Had that crack about Nick been a joke?

They had a quick bar snack in the hotel before going back to work. They managed to get a table in the window looking out over the River Thames. The sky was a delicate, shimmering silver-grey; light spilled down from behind a bank of thin cloud, giving the surface of the water a dancing glitter, as if a million herrings swam across it.

The river was busy today, lots of activity going on, lots to look at: a largish yacht moving down-river, white sails flapping; a string of tarpaulin-draped barges slowly chugging along, a shabby freighter with seagulls flapping around it coming up-river from the sea.

Gina stared out of the window, feeling bleak and weary, unaware of Roz watching her with a frown.

'What's wrong, Gina?'

Starting, she looked round. 'Nothing.' But her smile quivered and her green eyes were wide and glazed with unshed tears.

'Oh, come on,' Roz said gently, patting her hand. 'You can talk to me, you know that. We've known each other too long for me to miss the signs. How many years is it? So long, I forget. But all through school we were best friends, weren't we? When did that change? You're still my best friend—aren't I yours any more?'

Half laughing, half crying, Gina punched her shoulder. 'Oh, shut up! You know you are.'

'Hey, you don't know your own strength! I won't be able to use my keyboard for days,' Roz said, massaging her shoulder, then she said coaxingly, 'Well, come on, it helps to talk. Think I'm blind? Think I don't know when you're miserable? What is it? Nick?'

Gina's mouth went crooked. 'Why does it always have to be a man?'

'Don't ask me. I'm not God, I didn't invent them. God just had an off day.' Roz grinned at her. 'It is Nick, isn't it? What's he done to you? Is there someone else?'

Gina shook her head. 'I don't think so. It's just that he's angry because I wouldn't spend Christmas with him.'

'You didn't tell me he'd asked you to!' Roz's eyes opened wider. 'And you turned him down to spend it with us? Personally, I'm flattered, but I can see he wouldn't like the rejection. He isn't used to it. I did warn you what he was like.'

'You warned me,' agreed Gina, laughing shakily, and Roz stared into her green eyes and suddenly gave a long sigh.

'Oh, Gina, you do have it badly, don't you? Nick Caspian is not a safe man to love as much as that.'

Gina's face burned and she looked down, her lashes quivering against her hot cheek. What could she say in answer to that? She couldn't deny it—Roz knew her too well—and what she had said about Nick was only too true. Nick was not a safe man to love as much as she did, or to hate as much as she did. She wished with wrenching anguish that she could do one or the other— love or hate. Not both, at the same time. She felt like someone being pulled in two directions at once. Someone being slowly torn apart, limb from limb, by wild horses.

Nick got back from lunch with the Minister for Trade very late that afternoon, keeping Guy Faulkner, who had an appointment with him at four o'clock, waiting for twenty minutes.

After fifteen minutes he looked at the clock and said curtly, 'Is there any point in me waiting any longer? I have a lot to do this afternoon; I can't afford to waste time sitting here.'

Gina and Hazel looked at him, then at Sophie, who gave him an unhappy look.

'I'm sorry, Guy, I've no idea what's keeping him!'

He got to his feet. Gina quickly asked him, 'Have you sorted out your secretarial problems to your satisfaction?'

'Well, at least the new girl can spell, even if she isn't exactly pretty!'

Gina and Hazel grinned, exchanging looks. Sophie blushed, knowing what they were thinking, but Guy talked on, apparently blissfully unaware of all this amusement.

'The other one drove me crazy—whenever I went in to her office she was either talking to her boyfriend on the phone or doing her make-up or her nails. Work was the last thing on her agenda.'

'Never mind, Sophie sorted it out for you, didn't she?' said Hazel innocently and Guy nodded, turning to smile at Sophie.

'As usual. I'll never forgive you, Hazel, for talking her into taking your job. I'll never get another secretary as good as her.'

'Poor Guy,' Gina said, trying not to laugh, and then Nick strode into the room, like the north wind blowing through the city, and Guy was swept up with him and carried off.

At the door Nick paused and looked back at the three women. 'Gina, you had better sit in on this one!' His mouth twisted sarcastically. 'As you seem so interested in Tom Birny's latest crusade.' The cold grey eyes flicked on to Sophie and his tone warmed slightly. 'Bring us all some tea, will you, please, Sophie?'

'Yes, sir,' she said, almost curtsying. Sophie was treating Nick with awed, nervous respect; Gina knew she was terrified of him and no wonder, when he had been in a filthy mood ever since Sophie started work up here. It wasn't surprising that Sophie often wished she had never accepted the job; the rise in salary and status had tempted her, but she would much rather have gone on working for Guy. Hesitating, she had asked Gina for advice and Gina had told her frankly that it wasn't a good idea for lovers or husband and wife to go on working together. The private relationship often got in the way of the work.

Gina had thought grimly at the time, I should know! She found it very difficult to work with Nick.

In his office he threw himself into his leather chair, leaning back, his dark grey striped jacket flicked open to reveal the smooth-fitting matching waistcoat over a maroon-striped shirt. Loosening his maroon silk tie, Nick gave a long sigh of weariness.

'I'm sorry I'm late, Faulkner. Long dull lunch, couldn't get away. Now, let's have the latest on the East End families saga.'

Guy opened the fat folder he held and began to read a series of letters from solicitors. Sophie brought in the tray of tea and poured three cups. Gina watched, rather enviously, as Sophie gave a cup to Guy, their fingers touching, lingering. The two of them smiled at each other, their eyes bright, and Gina looked down, pain and longing aching inside her.

Sophie went out and Nick picked up his tea and sipped it, before asking tersely, 'Is that it, Faulkner?'

Guy shook his head. 'I wish it were. No, the legal side isn't bothering me—I doubt very much if they will sue because the last thing they want is to open up that particular can of worms. It would be an invitation to the police to investigate them.'

'The police should be doing that now!' Nick bit out, and Guy nodded drily.

'Of course, but it isn't as easy as it sounds. Some people will talk to Tom who wouldn't talk to the police. Tom comes from the East End, he grew up with these men, went to school with them. If he hadn't been a brilliant sportsman and escaped along that road, made plenty of money, then gone into journalism, he might have become a criminal.'

Nick laughed, startled and amused. 'You think so? I don't see Birny pulling off a bank robbery, somehow.'

'Don't be so sure. He's brave, ready to try anything, and he has brains of the right sort for crime. He's quick-thinking and shrewd, streetwise. I think he could have been very successful in crime.'

Nick gave Guy a faintly incredulous look. 'The way you talk, anyone would think it was a job like any other!'

'In some parts of London that's just what it is! You could even call it a career, and, as Tom is showing in these articles, it runs in families. People inherit family businesses that don't pay tax, don't issue dividends, but which make a great deal of money in a very illicit way. Tom really understands these people. He can get them to open up to him, where the police haven't a hope in hell of making them talk. At my suggestion, he submitted his articles to the police before we published; and they claim they're looking into his allegations——'

'About time too!' Nick said with angry contempt.

Guy's calm face was unchanged. 'Yes, well ... Tom may be right in his veiled accusations about police reluctance to act. Who knows why? Fear? Bribery? Or a feeling that the devil they know is better than a vacuum into which something worse might move? Whatever the reason, these gangs have flourished for far too long, without any determined attempt by the police to stamp them out. But there's no proof the police have just ignored them—so I had to get him to tone down his hints on that.'

Guy closed the folder and looked up, his face sombre, meeting Nick's intent eyes.

'As I say, I shall be amazed if anyone does take this to court. No, what's really worrying me is the private threats, aimed at Tom; at the *Sentinel*.' He paused, then added gravely, 'And at you, Mr Caspian.'

CHAPTER THREE

GINA went home early that evening; she had been invited to dinner by the wife of one of the directors and wanted to have a bath and dress before she had to drive back across town to the north, to Highgate, one of the older suburbs, full of expensive and beautiful houses with largish gardens and tree-lined streets, perched up on a hill overlooking the city. It was a short drive, but traffic made it difficult and she would need to leave herself plenty of time.

Her daily cleaner had left the place spotless, as usual, but although the apartment shone and was full of the scent of flowers in every room, not to mention beeswax polish, Gina felt very lonely that evening. The rooms echoed, emptily. Standing by the enormous windows, she looked over London's glitter and felt as if she was living on the moon.

Giving herself a shake, she went into the kitchen to make herself some lemon tea, then went to take her bath. Lying back in the fragrant water, drinking her tea, she thought about Nick, remembering with a pang Guy Faulkner's warning. He had been grave, but Nick had merely laughed.

'I get a death threat about once a week from someone!' he had mocked, and Gina had been startled and alarmed. Once a week! Ice had trickled down her back. It only needed one among those threats to be serious...

'It isn't funny!' she had burst out, and Nick had turned sharply to look into her dilated green eyes.

'Especially when you're one of those who'd like to see me dead!'

Gina had turned white at the bitter tone, the hostile stare, and Guy had looked startled for a second, but, recovering quickly, he had intervened with his usual discretion to smooth the moment over.

'I think the threats sent to Tom Birny should be taken very seriously. He obviously knows too much. For the moment, I think he should be got out of London. Maybe we could send him on holiday for a few weeks, until this blows over?'

Nick had slowly nodded. 'I take your point. We don't want him ending up as one of the crime statistics. He's too good a reporter to lose like that.'

He had stood up then, making it clear that the interview was at an end, and Guy had taken the hint and left. Gina had followed close on his heels without looking back. There was no point in trying to talk to Nick yet. How could she ask him to relent towards Hazel and Piet when he was so antagonistic towards *her*?

She had finished her tea. Her bathwater was lukewarm now. Gina sighed and climbed out of her bath, towelled briefly before slipping into a towelling robe and making her way to the bedroom.

She was half-dressed, in matching black silk bra, panties and slip, when the doorbell went. She froze, her green eyes dark and wide as she stared at her reflection in the dressing-table mirror. She knew who that was; it could only be Nick. The concierge would have rung first, to announce anyone else. Only Nick lived on this floor.

He rang again, sharply. Gina looked desperately around for her négligé. She couldn't go to the door half-naked. She tied the wide sash belt as she hurried along the corridor.

Nick was either on his way in or out: wearing his outdoor clothes, smooth black cashmere coat, a dark olive Paisley-pattern scarf around his neck, tucked into the V of his lapels. His skin glowed with the cold night air, his black hair was brushed smoothly flat. The impact of his presence hit Gina like a blow in the stomach; she was suddenly dry-mouthed.

While she was looking at him, those grey eyes coldly flicked over her, from her bare pink feet up to her damp hair. She clutched her négligé closer, trembling.

'Am I interrupting something?' he bit out and for a second she didn't get what he meant, then she flushed angrily.

'I was getting dressed!'

'After doing what?' he asked sardonically, his mouth twisting as he glanced past her into the apartment. 'And with whom?'

Gina was shaking with rage now. 'You've got a one-track mind! Is that all you came here for—to insult me? Because I'm not going to stand here listening, I haven't got the time. I'm in a hurry, I'm having dinner with the Calverts, and I have to be there by seven-thirty.'

She started to shut the door, and he put his foot in it, jamming it. Dark red crawled up his face; he didn't meet her eyes, muttering, 'Wait! Gina, I'm sorry. Seeing you looking so... Do you know how you look? God, Gina, I'm only human. The way you look at the moment, I can't help thinking... Well, how do I know if you're seeing anyone else? Philip Slade, Mac Cameron...you're always going out with other men; how do I know what you get up to with them? You're a beautiful, sexy woman; most men would love to make it with you. It's not surprising my imagination runs riot.'

'Well, I'm alone,' she said, hardly able to breathe properly. 'Are you going to believe me, or do you want to search the apartment?' She flung the door wide, gesturing angrily.

'Of course I believe you!' Nick took a step towards her, reached out a hand, touched her arm, his palm cold through the chiffon, against her warm flesh. Gina shivered at that touch and began trembling, her heartbeat so fast that it deafened her. Nick's eyes, his voice, were those of a man tortured by jealousy. She had often suspected him of lying to her, but she didn't think that tonight. He couldn't be acting. Unless he was another Laurence Olivier.

'What are you doing here, Nick?' she whispered.

'Well, I didn't call in here just to insult you!' His face was still darkly flushed, his eyes half hidden by lowered lids, only a silvery gleam betraying that he was watching her. 'I was on my way out to dinner, at the Russian embassy,' he said, the hand on her arm smoothing the sleeve of the négligé in an absent-minded way, as if he didn't realise he was doing it. 'Then I remembered...I wanted to check that everything was arranged for Hazel's party tomorrow night.'

'Yes, everything's fine.' Gina was intensely aware of his hand on her arm, the stroking movements of those long, slim fingers.

'Good. I've been so busy that I haven't had a chance to talk to you about it.' Nick shifted as if about to leave, but didn't go. His lids were still half lowered, but she felt his eyes restlessly moving up and down, over her; from her pale, bare throat to the creamy breasts the black chiffon covered but didn't conceal.

'Roz and I have been over every detail; don't worry, the party will work like clockwork,' she said huskily.

'You look very sexy in that thing,' Nick suddenly said, his voice low and very deep.

Gina's colour deepened. Her mouth was too dry for her to get a word out. The hand on her arm slid down and caressed her breast, his fingers splayed, moving, stroking.

'Gina...' he muttered.

Gina's pulses were going crazy, and her skin burned where his hand rested, but she fought to hide her instinctive reaction to his touch. The last thing she wanted was for Nick to know he could do that to her.

'Don't,' she said, pushing his hand away and looking down.

He drew an audible breath; through her lashes Gina saw his skin redden angrily, and she tensed, expecting another fierce outburst, but he had himself under control a moment later, his face tightening, his jaw clenched.

In a brusque voice he said, 'Sorry, I forgot you hated me to touch you! I'll be going. I have to be out of the office all morning tomorrow, so I'll see you at the party.'

He turned to leave and Gina suddenly remembered Hazel's anxious pleading, and caught hold of his arm.

'Wait, Nick...'

He looked down at the hand on his arm, his face savagely ironic. 'It's OK for you to touch me, is it? But not the other way around?'

She snatched her hand away as if from the touch of flame. 'I have to talk to you before you go,' she shakily muttered. 'If you could spare a moment?'

His eyes narrowed, searching her face. 'What about?'

'I can't talk to you out here. Come in for a moment, I won't keep you long.'

His mouth sneered. 'Sure you'll feel safe, alone with me in your flat?' His hard eyes flicked over her again, an insulting intimacy in the stare. 'Especially only wearing that!'

'Oh, stop it, Nick!' Gina's voice was raw with anger, with pain, with weariness.

There was a little silence while Nick stared at her, then he walked past her without another word. In the sitting-room, Gina faced him, pale and defiant, holding her négligé lapels together.

She moistened her dry lips with her tongue-tip, swallowed, then plunged straight into what she had to say. 'I know it was a shock to you when Hazel and Piet gave notice—Piet has worked for you for such a long time, it's understandable that you should be shaken when he says he is leaving—but...' She risked looking up, into his hard-bitten face, her green eyes pleading.

His features were grimly set. 'Did they ask you to talk to me? Why couldn't they do it themselves? Why ask you to?'

'I think they've tried, haven't they, Nick?' she said quietly, then, 'Nick, please ... can't you understand how Piet feels?' Her voice was soft, coaxing. For Hazel's sake, she had to get through to him. 'He wants to build up a firm of his own, to be independent, have something to leave his children. You can surely understand that?'

'I don't have any children!' He was scowling now, and Gina felt like hitting him.

'Don't be so irritating!' she burst out. 'You know what I mean. It's very upsetting for both of them, Hazel and Piet, to have you treating them like traitors. As if they had no right to strike out on their own...' She remembered what Hazel had said and quoted her, 'You're behaving as if they were runaway slaves.'

'What?' Nick snarled, making her jump.

She took a step backwards, trembling. 'I mean...after all, Piet has worked hard for you for years——'

'And I paid him a very good salary for it! Slaves don't get paid like that.'

She saw she had touched him on a nerve, and huskily said, 'I didn't say you treated him like a slave when he worked for you, but... Oh, Nick, can't you be more understanding? How would you like to have to work for someone else all your life? Caspian International means more to you than anything else in the world. Why shouldn't Piet be allowed to build up a company he can be proud of?'

Nick stared down at her, his face harsh, then suddenly turned on his heel and strode towards the front door. Gina slowly followed, her heart sinking. He refused to listen—he wasn't going to forgive Hazel and Piet, and she had wasted her time and energy trying to make him understand.

Before she reached it, the front door had slammed and he had gone. Tears sprang into her eyes, and she leaned on the wall, shuddering, for a moment, fighting to regain control.

She had to pull herself together, though; she had to finish getting ready and then drive to Highgate through heavy traffic. All the way there she kept thinking about Nick and trying to evict him from her mind. He was very hard to evict, however. He kept coming back, like a song.

The dinner party was larger than she had expected, but she knew most of the other guests, several of whom were fellow directors on the board of the *Sentinel*, and their wives were all women she had at least seen before at other functions of this sort.

Terry Calvert, a short, balding man with cheerful dark eyes, introduced her to one man she had never met before but who, she realised, had been invited tonight to partner her. 'This gorgeous creature is Gina Tyrrell, Mark. Gina, my nephew, Mark Calvert. Mark is an advertising executive with New Universe.'

'New Universe?' Gina repeated, offering her hand in some doubt.

Taking it, in a firm grip, the tall, dark-eyed Mark said, 'No need to look alarmed—I'm not an extra-terrestrial.' He gave her a teasing grin. 'We got the name through a merger—I used to work for a firm called New Adman, it was bought out by a firm called Universal Packaging, so they mixed the names up and emerged as New Universe Advertising.' He drew her down beside him on the couch he had been sitting on. 'Now, you tell me all about yourself. I gather from my uncle that you're a fellow director of his.'

'That's right.'

He looked her over with bright interest, from her gleaming russet hair, her full, soft mouth, along the lines of her nicely curved body in the full-skirted black lace cocktail dress she wore. 'You don't look like a company director, I must say!'

'We don't all come out of the same mould!' she said with mild irritation.

'Sorry, I was making glib assumptions and you can hit me if you like!' he said, and gave her a slow smile loaded with charm. Gina knew it was deliberate but she couldn't help smiling back. He had such nice eyes!

'Careful, I might take your offer up!'

He leaned closer, offering her his chin, and she pretended to punch it.

'Now you have to kiss it better,' he softly said, leaning even closer.

'I'm going to have to watch you!' said Gina, and then Mrs Calvert invited them to come to the table, and Mark took Gina's arm.

'They've put us together,' he said, cocking a lively eye at her. 'As you'll have noticed, we're the only couple under fifty and not married.'

Gina looked around the table a moment later, realising he was right, and Mark winked at her.

'Do you get the same feeling as me? That we're the victims of matchmaking?'

Gina pretended to think that was a joke, gave him a bright smile and changed the subject, but, in fact, feeling Mrs Calvert's satisfied gaze on her, she certainly did get that feeling. It happened to her all the time. Friends and acquaintances were always trying to find a suitable husband for her. She was a widow, therefore people assumed she must be on the look-out for a man. She found it infuriating and embarrassing, especially when she sensed that their motives were not entirely altruistic; she had inherited the Tyrrell money and that made her a big prize on the marital market.

At least with Mark Calvert that couldn't be true. His family were very rich indeed. He would not need to marry money; he would inherit a large country estate and a big house, one day.

The first course was put in front of them, a delicately flavoured beef consommé. Gina was grateful for the distraction. Now she could concentrate on the food instead of having to talk—and the food was well worth concentrating on!

'Delicious—I wish I could cook something like that!' she said politely to Mark, after the first course, and he nodded.

'It was good, wasn't it? My aunt uses a home chef operation; they bring the food to your house, cook it, serve it, and wash up afterwards, so all you have to do is enjoy the evening. It makes giving dinner parties very easy.'

'I must get their telephone number,' said Gina, and several other women who had been listening echoed her.

'Do you cook, Gina?' asked one of them, and Gina turned to talk to her across the table.

For most of the evening the talk was wide-ranging, from the current hits in the cinema to the latest weather report. It was while they were drinking their coffee that someone said, 'I called in and saw Dermot this morning.'

Everyone stopped talking and exchanged guarded looks, and Gina saw suddenly that they all knew about Sir Dermot's conspiracy against Nick. Nobody wanted to talk about it, for fear of possible consequences—and yet they were all dying to talk about it, she realised, from their expressions. Maybe they would have done, if Gina hadn't been there. As it was, Terry Calvert changed the subject and the polite small talk flowed on again, and after that nobody mentioned anything to do with Caspian International.

Although Mark Calvert was a lively and amusing companion, Gina left early, convinced that as soon as she was out of the way the men would all start talking about Sir Dermot and the plot to oust Nick from the *Sentinel*.

The odd little incident was another straw in the wind. Gina was beginning to feel very uneasy. What exactly was Sir Dermot plotting? Had he told her the whole truth? Or was he keeping something from her? And if so, what?

Next day, she saw nothing of Nick all morning. As he had told her, he was out of the office until after lunchtime, and when he came back he was closeted with a succession of senior executives on business.

Gina went straight to the Barbary Wharf hotel from work, at six o'clock, with Hazel, who was already laden with presents people had brought into the office all day. They both changed in the hotel room Gina had booked for herself for the night.

When the party started, it was a shock to Gina to see Tom Birny come wandering in with some of his friends from the newsroom.

'I thought you were going away for some weeks!' she said to him, and he gave her a cheerful grin.

'Oh, Guy's just being a bit jumpy. There's nothing to worry about—he shouldn't take these threats at face value. It's mostly bluff. They're hoping to scare me into shutting up, but they won't send a hitman to rub me out, don't worry.' And he roared with laughter at the very idea.

Gina gazed up at him, wide-eyed. He certainly didn't look like a man under sentence of death. He was taking the whole thing very lightly. No doubt Tom had often been threatened in the past, but Gina couldn't help being afraid that this time the men he had crossed were far more dangerous. Judging on his own articles, these men had killed before and would coolly kill again.

'Tom, please be careful!' she said and he nodded, still laughing.

'Well, I won't be walking around the East End after dark, I promise you! I'll take sensible precautions. Excuse me, Gina, I want to give Hazel a kiss and the present I brought her.'

He walked away, still smiling, and Gina stared after him, her face anxious. She liked Tom Birny; he always reminded her of a big, friendly puppy and she hated the thought of anything happening to him.

'Penny for your thoughts!'

Piet's voice made her jump and she turned, hurriedly smiling. 'They aren't worth it. It's so good to see you, Piet. You look very fit, as usual—all that fresh air you get, I suppose! How do you think Hazel is looking?'

'Beautiful,' he said simply, looking across the room towards his wife, who was opening Tom Birny's present and exclaiming over the very pretty pale yellow baby clothes she found. 'Being pregnant suits her.'

'You sound surprised about that!' Gina said rather wryly, and Piet laughed with an expression of self-derision.

'I suppose I am. I was not too keen on her having a baby at all, but I'm changing my mind more and more every day. It's fun, looking forward to being a father.'

Gina smiled at him. 'You don't know how much I envy the two of you!'

Piet's face turned serious, he looked down at her gently. 'It will happen for you, one day soon, Gina.' He hesitated. 'I thought . . . maybe . . . you and Nick . . .'

She blushed hotly. 'No!'

Piet sighed. 'No, Hazel says you will not forgive him for what happened to Sir George. This seems sad to me. I have always felt you two were suited.'

Her green eyes flashed. 'Please, Piet, I don't want to talk about it! Tell me about your new home, in Middelburg. Is it near your sister's place?'

He nodded. 'Very near. I planned it this way because quite often I shall be away and Hazel would be alone with the baby, and having my sister near by will make it easier for her.'

'That's very thoughtful of you. I know Hazel likes your sister and her family very much.'

'I want her to be happy,' Piet said in his careful English. 'You know, it has not been easy for either of us to be apart since we got married. I wish most of all that I could have been with her throughout her pregnancy. I've missed out on a lot by being in Holland while she's over here.'

'Never mind, you can be there all the time when she has the next one!'

Piet's blue eyes widened in horror. 'Next one! You don't think she'll want any more for years, do you?'

'Don't ask me, ask Hazel!' Gina said, laughing at his expression. 'But I think somehow that she'll be too busy with this baby to want any more for quite a while.'

Piet sighed. 'Well, I hope so. Hazel has convinced me that we can easily work together and keep an eye on the baby at the same time, but if we had any more things would get complicated.' He paused, then asked, 'Did she tell you that when she went for her last scan they offered to tell her the baby's sex, but she refused?'

Gina nodded. 'She prefers to wait to find out.'

Piet shook his head wryly. 'Women are baffling. I would have loved to know. I'm dying to find out if it is a boy or a girl.'

'Ah, but Hazel has to carry it for another couple of months—I can see why she'd rather not know until the birth. It makes the waiting easier, gives her something to look forward to! It's a bit like unwrapping a Christmas present in advance. It spoils the day itself if you do.'

Piet did not look convinced, but he smiled. 'Well, whenever the baby does arrive I hope you will come and

visit us to see it, whatever it is! I know Hazel is going
to miss you. You will keep in touch, won't you, Gina?'

'Of course I will!'

'Thank you.' Piet's eyes grew sad. 'I wish we could
part with Nick on such good terms, but I've committed
the one unforgivable sin in his eyes. I'm walking away
from him.'

'I talked to him yesterday, Piet, but I'm not too
hopeful that he listened!'

Piet nodded, grimacing. 'That was very good of you,
Gina. Thank you. It doesn't surprise me to hear he
wouldn't listen. Nick doesn't take rejection lightly; he
never forgives anyone who walks out on him.'

'Because of his childhood,' Gina said quietly, and Piet
gave her a grim smile, nodding.

'You worked that out? That is very shrewd of you,
Gina. Of course. Oh, it is buried so deep inside his psyche
that he doesn't even understand it himself—but between
them his parents have made Nick hypersensitive about
any sort of rejection, however slight or meaningless.
That's what makes him so insistent on winning when he
makes a bid for a new company, so some consequences
of his paranoia are quite productive.' Piet laughed a little
bitterly.

'It makes him obsessive, too,' said Gina. 'And that
can be frightening!'

Piet watched her, frowning. 'I have sometimes thought
that if he found the right woman this anger inside him
might die down. What Nick needs is to be loved as he
wasn't loved when he was a child, I think.'

'His mother loved him, and still does!' Gina protested.

'Oh, yes, you have met her, I think?' Piet said
thoughtfully. 'Nick mentioned that you were going with
him on one of his trips to San Francisco. I have seen
that extraordinary house she lives in! An architect of
genius, but a little mad, I think. Not that that detracts
anything from his work. I know some sane architects

whose work is as dull as ditchwater! So, what did you think of Mrs Caspian?'

'I liked her, didn't you?'

'She is charming,' Piet agreed. 'Very beautiful, even now that she is old, and not many beautiful women retain their beauty until that age!'

'And Nick loves her,' Gina said huskily. 'His paranoia doesn't include her. He doesn't blame her for his rather sad childhood; he realises it was his father who used his money and power to get him away from her, and she fought hard to keep him, you know. She didn't relinquish him easily.'

'No, but she did give him up, in the end, remember. Nick may know with his conscious mind that she had no other choice, but does his unconscious know that? The part of him that is still a child only remembers that she sent him away, that his father sent him off to a boarding-school where he was very unhappy, that nobody cared what happened to him.'

'It was all so long ago, though!'

'Time doesn't always heal, even though new skin grows over the wound. Nick's childhood is like a bruise buried deep under the skin. On the surface there is nothing to see, but if somebody touches it, however lightly, the pain comes back.'

Gina stared at Piet, dumbfounded by his understanding of Nick's feelings. He gave her a slow, wry smile.

'So be careful how you touch him, Gina,' he said, and at that moment there was a stir in the room, people turned to look towards the door, and Piet stiffened, staring.

'He's here! I'd started to think he wasn't going to turn up at all.'

Gina had also begun to be afraid of that; her eyes filled with relief as she glanced across the room to where Nick was talking to Hazel.

Nick was in evening dress; his broad shoulders and deep chest fitting smoothly under the well cut jacket, the dark material making him look taller than ever, elongating his lean, athletic body and those long, slim legs.

Hazel was radiant as he smiled down at her. Nick's appearance tonight had made her last day with the firm much happier. He gave her a gold-wrapped present. Hazel opened it, gave a little gasp, looked up at him, saying something breathless. Nick laughed and bent to kiss her, and Piet gave a long sigh.

'Well, he has forgiven Hazel, anyway!'

Gina gave him a little push. 'Go over there, talk to him—don't waste the opportunity!'

Piet took an uncertain step towards them just as Nick looked round. Piet stopped dead, watching Nick with tension in his pale face. Nick stared at him, then suddenly smiled.

Gina's eyes filled with tears. She would probably never know whether or not what she had said to him had had any effect on Nick, but she didn't care. The only thing that mattered was that he was here, and he was smiling at Piet; they were friends again.

Piet began to walk fast towards Nick, who came to meet him in the middle of the room and gave him a rough bear-hug, slapping his back.

'Good luck for the future. I'm going to miss you, damn you! But good luck, anyway.'

Gina turned away, got out her handkerchief discreetly, wiped her eyes, and blew her nose, then went over to join them. Hazel gave her a quivering smile.

'Look...Nick gave me this...'

Gina's mouth rounded. 'Oh, isn't that pretty!'

Nick hadn't bought Hazel baby clothes, or household items, as everyone else had done. He had given her a slim velvet box in which lay a diamond pendant, blazing whitish-blue, on a gold chain; with matching diamond earrings.

'I must have them insured before I wear them,' Hazel said with her usual practical good sense.

Gina looked at the time. 'Now that Nick's here, shouldn't we ask them to serve the buffet? I'll give the head waiter the signal.'

She had done the table seating plans: she had put Nick on the same table as herself, Piet and Hazel and several of the senior staff. Everyone else would have to queue up to get their food, but the top table would be served by waiters. Gina couldn't imagine Nick standing in line for a plate of chicken or salad, and it was out of the question for Hazel to stand for any length of time.

But Nick had other plans, she discovered a few moments later, as they moved towards the table with its neatly handwritten name tags before each place.

'Colette will sit with me,' he coolly said, pulling back the chair next to his, ignoring the place card bearing Gina's name—and only then did Gina realise that Colette Tse was with him.

Hazel shot Gina a startled, questioning look, obviously at a loss to know what to say.

Piet said quickly, 'The places are all arranged, Nick; someone else would have to move if Colette sat there.'

'Then someone else will have to move,' said Nick, unmoved.

Everyone at the table stood there, shuffling, very embarrassed, except Colette.

Almond eyes darkly gleaming, Colette sat down without any sign of confusion. Nick poured her a glass of the very good white wine which had been placed on the table, poured himself wine, tilted his glass towards her in a silent, intimate toast. Colette glowed: fine-boned and yet sinuously seductive in a lemon silk evening dress, a deep collar of pearls around her throat and pearl studs in her ears.

Gina turned and walked away blindly, hearing Hazel behind her call anxiously, 'Gina!' but ignoring it. She had her pride; Nick wasn't humiliating her and getting away with it.

She heard a whispering, sensed people staring at her. The other guests had begun to pick up on the fact that something odd was happening on the top table. Gina wished the floor would open up and swallow her. If she could only get out of here!

Then someone was in her way, she tried to side-step, muttering, 'Sorry,' without looking up, but two hands seized her arms and refused to let go when, startled, she tried to pull away.

Gina looked up, green eyes huge and brilliant with unshed tears. 'Oh . . . Tom . . .'

'Coming to slum with us workers, are you? That's right,' Tom said cheerfully, his voice pitched much louder than usual, deliberately meant to be overheard. 'That's the Tyrrell way! Sir George was never too proud to take his coat off, roll up his sleeves and work alongside the printers in the old Fleet Street days! Here, I've got you a plate of food, sit over here with me.'

Gratefully, Gina let him pull her over to one of the tables while dozens of pairs of eyes watched. As she sat down, Roz and Daniel arrived, carrying their plates, moving from another table to join her and Tom.

'Are you OK?' Roz whispered, face concerned.

'Fine,' Gina said, smiling much too brightly.

'What the hell was all that about?'

'She decided she'd rather sit with us,' Tom insisted, and Roz met his eyes and gave a wry, slow smile.

'Very sensible of her; we're much more fun!'

Daniel had filled a glass of wine; he put it into Gina's hand, patting her fingers affectionately.

'*Ça, c'est très bon, chérie. Buvez*!' Then, in English, 'A good wine always makes you feel better, you know!'

A little warmth crept back into her; at least she had good friends! She drank half the glass, while the others talked around her, and after a few minutes she was able to join in; laughing at Tom's awful jokes, telling Roz how chic she looked, asking Daniel about a story she had read on the Foreign page that morning. She chattered and sparkled, her green eyes very bright—and if there was something feverish about her gaiety none of them commented on it or even looked as if they had noticed.

CHAPTER FOUR

NICK left for Luxembourg the following day. Discovering this when she went into work next morning, Gina sat fuming at her desk, having worked herself into a state of angry energy in order to have a showdown with him and now having nothing to do with all that rage.

'He ran away!' Roz told her, amused, when they met for lunch at Pierre's later.

Startled, Gina looked across the table, green eyes wide. 'Do you think so?'

'It can't be a coincidence! Well, well, well. Nick Caspian running away from a confrontation! That must be a first. He's always thrived on fights.' Roz considered her thoughtfully, face shrewd. 'I tell you what, lovie—the man's scared of you. How does that make you feel?'

'Incredulous!' Gina couldn't help laughing at the very idea. She shook her head at Roz. 'No, I can't believe it. Nick, scared of me? That isn't very probable, is it?'

'Probable, maybe not,' agreed Roz, who was looking sleek and dynamic in a white leather jacket with a black silk tunic top under it, and a straight black skirt. 'All the same, I think I'm right. He hadn't mentioned a trip to Luxembourg in advance, had he?'

'He's always having to rush off there for one reason or another. He spends more time in Luxembourg than anywhere else. After all, that is his headquarters, the international corporation is run from there, it's the hub from which all the spokes radiate outwards, especially the financial affairs of Caspian International, and Nick makes sure he keeps a very close eye on those!'

'He has spent more time in London than anywhere else, over the past year, actually,' Roz thought aloud, watching her. 'And that isn't just because he has been overseeing the move to Barbary Wharf, or the overhaul of the *Sentinel*. Nick has stayed here because of you, and you know it.'

Gina flushed angrily. 'Oh? Really? So what was all that with Colette Tse?'

'Oh, for heaven's sake, Gina, isn't it obvious? He's trying to make you jealous.' Roz looked wryly at her. 'And he succeeded, didn't he?'

'No, he did not!' Her colour even deeper, Gina denied it fiercely. 'Jealous? You have to be kidding.' She pretended to laugh, but it wasn't very convincing, as Roz's cynical eyes told her. Defiantly she muttered, 'I don't give a damn how many women he has. The only thing I care about is the *Sentinel* and I hate what he is doing to it. He has to be stopped.'

That was the thought uppermost in her mind when, a few days later, she went to visit Sir Dermot Gaskell, now back home, his leg in plaster. He was looking much better than he had the last time she saw him, as she told him.

'Yes, I feel fine now,' he smiled. 'But I'm off to the Caribbean for a few weeks in the sun—that's what I really need. Some sunshine. I shall just relax in a chair by a pool and forget all about dreary old London.'

'When do you come back?'

'I haven't decided yet. Mid-February?'

'But when ... how soon do you think you'll be ready to launch an attack on Nick Caspian?'

Sir Dermot gave her a shrewd look, leaned over and patted her hand with fatherly kindness. 'I heard what happened at Hazel's farewell party. I'm not surprised you're furious. It was disgraceful. Deliberate, too, no doubt. I'd say he wants to push you out altogether. You're the last Tyrrell on the board, in the firm. Of course Caspian wants to get rid of you, and he chose to humiliate you in public in the hope of making you so mad you'd resign on the spot.'

That hadn't occurred to Gina and she frowningly stared into his face. 'No, I don't think so.'

'My dear, why else be so blatant about it? He had some motive for making such a public scene.'

'Yes,' she said slowly, biting her lip. Nick had wanted to hurt her, that was why! Or was she kidding herself? Had he had some other, secret motive? Did he want her out of the *Sentinel*, and off the board?

'At least this means you are a hundred per cent on our side,' Sir Dermot said with unhidden satisfaction. 'Don't worry, at the next board meeting, in mid-February, we'll hit him before he has an inkling what is going on. When I get back from my Caribbean trip, I'll throw a dinner party and we can all discuss our plans. Until then, be patient, my dear Gina.'

She managed a smile. 'OK, Sir Dermot.'

She glanced at the clock, preparing to leave, but Sir Dermot began speaking again, his face curious and amused.

'Tell me about this Chinese girl. A real beauty, I'm told. How long has his affair with her been going on? I hadn't heard a whisper, and my sources are usually very good.'

'I don't know anything about it,' Gina said in a tight, careful voice. 'Nor do I want to!'

That wasn't true, of course. She was eaten up with bitter curiosity, but she would have died rather than admit as much to anyone. Not that anybody dared mention it. Hazel might have done, if she had been there, but Gina was working with Sophie now, and, pleasant though she found her new colleague, there wasn't the same rapport, the same frank exchanges. Sophie was friendly and eager to say the right thing; she never mentioned Nick Caspian or Colette Tse, and nor did anybody else—at least, not to Gina's face.

Walking across the plaza next day, Gina heard somebody say Nick's name, and tensed, noticing two girls out of the corner of her eye, standing in front of Torelli's, looking at the food in the window. Gina paused behind a palm tree to eavesdrop, kneeling down, pretending to be tightening a small bow on one of her black shoes.

'Is it true he's taken Colette Tse with him?' a small blonde girl asked, rather absently, her real interest on the display of salads. 'I like their crab salads; they're very low in calories but they're delicious, Maureen.'

'No, I'm having cheese and pickles, and damn the calories!' said the other, a plump brunette Gina recognised as one of the girls in the secretarial pool.

'Are you dumping your diet again, Maureen? Where's your will-power?'

'It's cold and I'm starving,' Maureen defiantly snapped back. 'Anyway, as I said, I was working in Accounts this morning, that little dark girl is off sick, the one with the very long hair and big teeth...'

'Jennifer?'

'No, Janet. Well, I'm doing her job until she's back—collating the editorial expenses sheet, and I tell you what, some of those reporters put in some amazing claims... talk about works of fiction! I'm glad I don't have to decide whether or not to pay up on them. Anyway, the whole office was talking about Nick Caspian and Colette Tse, and Rosie Lloyd said... you know Rosie...'

'I don't think so.'

'Yes, you do! Curls her hair herself and it uncurls as soon as we get a drop of rain.'

'Doesn't ring any bells with me!'

'Kay, don't be daft! You had a row with her in the canteen over the last piece of salmon and broccoli pie, last week!'

'Oh, her! I didn't know her name was Rosie. It doesn't suit her; she's too skinny and pale.'

'Yes, well, she said Colette had rung up from Luxembourg to say she was there on official business, it wasn't to come out of her leave—and she'd be away for a week! Well, obvious, isn't it, Kay? He's there, so is she! Don't need to be Sherlock Holmes to work that one out, do you?'

'I like her calling it official business!' the blonde girl said, chuckling.

'Maybe he sees it as part of her job! He looks as if he would be pretty ruthless, blackmail girls into bed without a blink.'

'He wouldn't need to blackmail me,' Kay said dreamily. 'Just a smile, that's all it would take! I think he's the sexiest guy I've seen in years.'

'Oh, you! You said that about Jack Harrison, in Accounts, and he's got a bald spot and wears horn-rimmed glasses!'

'But have you seen him going home on his motorbike in his black leathers? I can just imagine Nick Caspian in black leather... I bet he'd be a walking dream.'

'Oh, let's order our lunch,' Maureen said, laughing. 'Or you'll be too excited to eat.'

They vanished into Torelli's and Gina stood up and walked slowly into the foyer. Her mind was in a state of wild confusion. Nick had taken Colette to Luxembourg with him?

She acted like a robot, took the lift, up to her office, where she could be alone, because Sophie was out to lunch and wouldn't be back for half an hour, at least.

Gina shut the door and leaned on it, her eyes shut too. Oh, God... Nick with Colette... pain beat inside her, like terrified wings on the bars of a cage, as if her heart tried to escape her body, leave behind the grief and anguish of her thoughts. She couldn't even bear to imagine it. Yet, how to stop the images, the pictures of them both together? She remembered Nick's lean, powerful body naked in her own arms, the heat and passion of his searching mouth, the aching sweetness as he arched above her, in her, moving with her.

Gina groaned aloud, doubling up in agony, her arms across her stomach as if she had cramp. 'Oh, Nick, Nick,' she hoarsely breathed, then bit her lip so hard that a little spot of blood appeared on the pink flesh.

No. Don't think, don't imagine it, she ordered herself. But the visions still came, torturing her. The very idea of him touching Colette like that was intolerable. He belonged to her. The word surprised her—she had never admitted she felt like that before, even to herself, in the privacy of her thoughts. That was how she felt, though. Nick was hers; he belonged to her, as if he had her personal stamp on his forehead. Gina remembered the poet Wyatt who had loved Anne Boleyn yet known that she was giving herself to King Henry the Eighth. '*Noli me tangere*, for Caesar's I am,' Wyatt had said, in his bitter, tragic poem to his lost love. 'Touch me not, for I am Caesar's,' was graven with diamonds around her neck.

Gina felt that that was the way she belonged to Nick, and Nick to her. And she wished violently that there were some way to get that message across to Colette.

How could she, though? Nick was not her property, he could do as he chose, and, apparently, he had chosen to take Colette to Luxembourg and ...

Think about something else! she hurriedly told herself, but her thoughts would only go round in a circle. Why had she been left to find out that way, eavesdropping on two girls she only knew by sight? Nobody had breathed a word to her, not even Roz—but everyone must have known. Except her. They must all have been talking about it endlessly, but when she was around they would hurriedly change the subject, talk of other things, while secretly they watched her, knowing they knew something she didn't know. Did they enjoy the sense of power that secret knowledge gave them? Was that why they had been silent?

No, not Roz, she thought. Roz didn't say anything because she couldn't bring herself to tell me; she knew how much it was going to hurt me. And that was another humiliation, on top of all the others she had suffered lately. It made it worse to know that Roz understood what she was going through!

Gina drew herself up, lifting her russet head in a defiant little jerk. She couldn't stop Roz guessing how she felt, but she didn't have to let Roz see! Nobody must see anything. From now on she must be on her guard against prying eyes, curious eyes, even those of friends who loved her and cared what happened to her.

Damn Nick Caspian. From now on, she was wholeheartedly behind Sir Dermot and his conspirators. In fact, she couldn't wait to see Nick's face when the bomb exploded underneath him!

A few days later she had a phone call from his secretary in Luxembourg that Nick was on his way back to London, but before his plane had touched down another message arrived, this time for Nick.

Sophie took it while Gina was out, and was in a most unusual state for her, almost approaching panic, when Gina walked in after lunch.

'Oh, thank heavens you're back!' she said, looking so very un-cool that Gina felt a stab of real alarm.

'Why? What's happened?'

'I've been trying to get hold of you, I rang Roz and she said you were shopping in the West End...'

'Sophie, take a deep breath and start again—why were you looking for me, and what's wrong?'

Sophie took a breath, sighed. 'I had a message half an hour ago saying that Mrs Caspian was arriving at

Heathrow at four, and would Nick meet her plane? I rang Luxembourg, but...'

'He had left,' nodded Gina. 'He's on his way here.'

'So his secretary said. I asked her to get a message to him on his plane, but she thought he might have landed by now and she wasn't sure how to get in touch with him. She suggested we might have his car phone number here, and I've been looking through his records but I can't find it.'

'It must be in there somewhere,' Gina said, frowning, going over to the filing cabinets to check Nick's personal file. Over her shoulder, she said, 'In any case, he was flying to Gatwick and stopping off en route to see Sir Alfred Petworth, the paper manufacturer, who lives near there. After that, he was flying to London in a helicopter and landing at the docklands airport, so he wouldn't be in any position to meet Mrs Caspian's plane.'

She hunted through the thick file, while Sophie watched, hovering behind her. After a moment Gina slammed the drawer shut.

'Found it?' asked Sophie hopefully.

'No.' Gina turned, looking uncertain. 'What I can't understand is why his mother didn't let him know when she was coming. She must be using their private jet; Nick wouldn't have her using the ordinary airlines. Did she say which terminal? I suppose it must be either Terminal Three or Four, as it's from the States. It seems very odd; Mrs Caspian so rarely travels. She's a semi-invalid.'

Sophie stared, her eyes rounding. 'Gina! It wasn't those terminals, it was Terminal Two, a flight from Italy. Maybe it isn't his mother!'

'But you said Mrs Caspian! As far as I know there's only one Mrs Caspian, and that's...' Gina's voice trailed off and she went white.

'Unless he has got married!' Sophie was breathless with excitement. 'He doesn't have a brother, does he?'

'No,' whispered Gina.

'Or a married uncle? I mean, this couldn't be his aunt? Or some other relative?'

'As far as I know he only has two sisters. I suppose you could have misheard the name. It could be Miss Caspian—one of them isn't married.'

'It was a fax, Gina, I didn't hear it, it was printed out—Mrs Caspian. Here, take a look!'

Gina looked at the torn off strip of paper. 'Yes, well, I've never heard of another Mrs Caspian.' She forced a pathetic pretence of laughter. 'Unless, as you say, he's secretly married.'

'But he couldn't keep a marriage secret for long, could he? Someone would have found out. Of course it could just have happened.' Sophie paused, mouth wide open, very flushed, then gabbled, 'Oh! Maybe that's why he...' Her voice trailed off again, but Gina knew how she would have finished the sentence.

Maybe that was why Nick had taken Colette Tse to Luxembourg with him? Maybe they had flown there to get married?

Gina had never believed that hearts could break, but something agonising was happening inside her chest. It felt as if her heart was breaking. It hurt that much.

She tried to think practical, sensible, down-to-earth thoughts. Why should Nick have flown all that way to get married in secrecy? It didn't make sense. Or did it?

Nick was not a British subject, and nor, she thought, was Colette. Gina couldn't remember. If she had ever known for sure. She barely knew Colette. Nor did Nick, she feverishly told herself. Until the last week or so Nick had never shown any signs of being interested in Colette, except as a very talented features editor.

But they were as likely to get married in Luxembourg as anywhere else, especially since Caspian International was based there. Maybe it made some sort of financial sense to get married there? No doubt Nick would have

a very good reason for choosing Luxembourg. It
probably helped tax-wise!

Gina laughed wildly, and met Sophie's eyes. Sophie
was looking at her oddly: her lower lip caught between
her teeth, making her look like a nibbling mouse, thought
Gina in a strange, close-to-the-edge mood.

She knew what was going on in Sophie's mind. Sophie
had just remembered the company gossip that she and
Nick had once been an item and were still somehow involved, although more in quarrelling than lovemaking.
So far as anyone knew. Sophie was embarrassed now,
and sympathetic. Her eyes said, Poor Gina! Is she
hurting?

Well, yes! Gina *was* hurting, thank you very much,
Sophie. Gina was hurting like hell, and angry because
her pain couldn't be hidden, because Sophie was here
to witness it and be sorry for her. Gina could do without
pity; it stung like the bite of a scorpion. She had to break
the atmosphere up before Sophie actually said something kind and gentle, something Gina would find it hard
to forgive.

'No, joking aside, it must be his mother,' she said,
laughing again. 'And someone must be at Heathrow to
meet her. I'll go. If Mr Caspian comes straight here from
the airport, tell him I've gone, and say I'll escort Mrs
Caspian to his apartment.'

She drove to Heathrow in an official company car,
driven by a company chauffeur, but there was so much
traffic on the motorway heading out of London that they
only just got to the airport in time. Gina's nerves were
jumping under her skin like ants by the time she walked
across the crowded terminal, paused to check a com-
puterised Arrivals board.

The only possible plane arriving from Italy at the right
time was one from Milan, and it had just touched down.
Of course, it was still possible that Mrs Caspian had
flown on Nick's private jet, but she would have to pass

through Passports and Customs before she could leave Terminal Two, so Gina positioned herself at the exit gate, her eyes flicking through face after face, waiting to find out if the mystery arrival was Nick's mother or...or someone else.

She was so tense that, in the end, she didn't even recognise Mrs Caspian until the older woman was almost in front of her, and then she did a double-take, gasping like a landed fish, and laughing a little wildly.

'Mrs Caspian...there you are! I didn't see you coming!'

She had forgotten just how beautiful Nick's mother still looked, with her fine, dark eyes and silvered jet-black hair. She was in her middle fifties, but Gina could have sworn she was ten years younger.

'Gina! How kind of you to meet me!' she said in her huskily lilting voice which in spite of her having lived in America for years still had a Spanish accent. She put both arms around Gina and kissed her on both cheeks in Continental style. 'You look even lovelier than I remembered! Your wonderful hair! Such fire.' She brushed a hand lightly over Gina's head, smiling, then looked around, faint puzzlement in her face. 'But where is Nick?'

Gina gave her an apologetic look. 'He was flying into Gatwick this afternoon and we couldn't reach him to give him your message, I'm afraid. Was he expecting you?'

Mrs Caspian smiled wryly. 'No, I came on impulse. I went to Italy, after Christmas, to spend the New Year with my daughter, who has been in Tuscany painting for some months now. Then we went to Milan to do some shopping, and yesterday I talked to Nick on the phone, he said he was coming back today, and Alessa and I decided to join him here.' She looked sideways and only then did Gina realise that there was someone with her, standing close to her, as if ready to put an arm around her if she needed it. A tall, slender, dark woman with a strong-boned face which was oddly familiar, the family resemblance quite striking, and quick, bright eyes which met Gina's with smiling friendliness.

'Gina,' Mrs Caspian said softly, 'this is my younger daughter, Alessa.'

Alessa held out a large, well-shaped hand. 'Hello, Gina, I've heard a lot about you!'

Gina was still staring as she shook hands. 'You're so like your brother!'

'Don't say that!' Alessa grimaced.

'She is, isn't she?' agreed Mrs Caspian, laughing, but as Gina gave her a smile she saw faint lines of weariness around her mouth and eyes.

'You must both be tired! The car is waiting just outside the doors; shall we go now?' She glanced at the airport trolley beside Alessa, on which stood four tan leather suitcases. 'Is that yours?' Even as she asked she saw the gold initials discreetly stamped on the side of the cases. 'I'll take care of them, shall I?'

She wheeled the trolley outside to where the grey limousine was waiting. The chauffeur jumped out and took charge of the cases, stowed them away deftly, in time to help Mrs Caspian into the back of the car. Alessa slid in beside her mother, and Gina took the front seat, next to the driver, to give them a little privacy, but spoke to them through the sliding glass window between the two parts of the vehicle.

'I imagine you will be staying with Nick?'

'Yes.' Mrs Caspian looked uncertainly at Gina. 'But if he is away the apartment would be locked up, wouldn't it?'

'You must use mine until he gets back; I've left a message at the office to tell him I'm meeting you, so he'll realise you're with me.'

Mrs Caspian glanced at Alessa, then back at Gina, smiling gratefully. 'That is very kind, Gina, are you sure? We could just as easily go to a hotel for tonight.'

'But I'd enjoy having you visit me! I have so few visitors, and after all I stayed with you in San Francisco and had a wonderful time in your beautiful home; I'll be glad to repay your hospitality. My apartment isn't as extraordinary as your house, just a modern penthouse suite, but I can boast a view almost as good as yours!' She told the chauffeur to drive to the apartment block on the riverside, and they set off along the busy motorway.

'I have not been to London for a long time,' said Mrs Caspian, looking out at the clogged traffic, the low-lying, scrubby fields on either side of the road. 'Has it changed much?'

'It changes all the time, but it stays the same, too— you'll recognise it. Do you know London, Alessa?'

'I came here once or twice, on summer trips, when I was at college, but I only stayed a few weeks. I have very happy memories of the English countryside, but I didn't spend much time in London. I'm looking forward to seeing Barbary Wharf; my brother and Piet van Leyden are so enthusiastic about the architecture.'

'Yes, it is very striking, if you like modern architecture,' Gina said wryly, and Alessa laughed, her dark eyes glinting.

'I gather you don't?'

'I'm never sure. I've got quite fond of it, working there throughout this year, but I must say I prefer traditional architecture.' She glanced out of the window as they passed through the outskirts of the London borough of Hammersmith. 'I'm afraid we have a long drive still ahead of us. As you'll remember, the apartment block is in the old dockland area of London, not very far from Barbary Wharf, so I'll ask the driver to make a detour to show you the complex. It won't add any time to our journey.'

Mrs Caspian had leaned back in the corner of the limousine, her head against the cushions and her eyes closed. Gina gave her an anxious look, then looked at Alessa enquiringly, raising her brows and silently mouthing, 'Is she OK?'

Alessa glanced at her mother, then back at Gina, nodding. 'Tired,' she mouthed mutely.

Gina softly said, 'Flying is always tiring. You must be tired, too; I'll let you have a rest until we get to Barbary Wharf.'

She turned round to face the way they were going, and nothing more was said until they were through the centre of London and driving along the river bank towards the dockland stretch. Gina waited until she saw Barbary Wharf looming up ahead of them, then turned to warn Alessa they were almost there.

Alessa sat forward, fascinated, as the car slowed on the approach to the complex. Gina looked, too, with new eyes because a stranger was staring at the place she now knew so well. She had to admit it was striking: the black and red brick walls, with a Greek key patterning in the bands, the black glass windows which mirrored the sky and even an aeroplane passing overhead at that moment, and gave the building a strangeness which was dreamlike, the octagonal structure which gave it the look of some medieval fortress, especially with the high, castellated walls surrounding it. There was no building in London like it; the complex was unique and faintly frightening, and like a medieval castle it had been built for a warlike purpose, to keep people out and protect what was inside.

'What do you think?' she asked Alessa, who was taking in the whole place, inch by inch, with narrowed, thoughtful eyes.

'It isn't a wallpaper building, is it?' Alessa obliquely commented.

'But do you like it?' Gina found herself really interested in the other woman's opinion. Alessa Caspian was Nick's sister, and Gina wanted to get to know her, understand her. It might help her to understand him.

'It's exciting,' Alessa said. 'Different. There's that little shock you get when you see something that surprises you.'

'The shock of the new?' Gina laughed, remembering the television programme on modern art which had had that title.

'Exactly. I can see why Piet was impressed. It's a dramatic statement about the nature of the workplace, and its style is confident, sure of itself, even a little arrogant.'

'Is that good or bad?' Gina asked, amused.

'There are no moral values in art,' Alessa said. 'You either like it or you don't; it either speaks to you, or it doesn't. This does. Yes, I like it.'

'So do I,' Mrs Caspian said, her eyes twinkling. She winked at Gina. 'I don't know if it speaks to me, mind you. Have you seen enough, Alessa? Can we get on now? I'm dying for a glass of hot milk and somewhere comfortable to put my feet up for an hour or two!'

Half an hour later, Gina showed Mrs Caspian into her spare bedroom. 'Would you like me to turn down the bed for you?' she asked, going to the windows to close the curtains.

'No, my dear, I won't get into bed. If you don't mind, could we take off this lovely quilt so that I can lie on top of the bedclothes?'

'Of course,' said Gina, deftly stripping off the quilt. 'But won't you want something over you? If you fall asleep your temperature will drop, and I wouldn't want you to catch cold. How about a blanket?' She went to a cupboard and produced a tartan blanket while Mrs Caspian took off her shoes and lay down. Gina spread the blanket over her, and Mrs Caspian smiled up at her, already drowsy-eyed.

'Thank you, Gina. That's perfect.'

Gina went to the door, clicked off the light. From the darkness behind her Mrs Caspian murmured sleepily, 'By the way, who is Colette Tse? Do you know her, Gina?'

Gina stiffened and took a deep breath to steady her voice before she answered. 'She's features editor of the *Sentinel*.'

'Chinese?'

'Half Chinese, half English.'

'Nick seems to think highly of her. Do you like her? Is she pretty?'

'She's beautiful,' Gina said carefully, and then she couldn't bear any more, so she went out and closed the door.

So Nick had talked about Colette to his mother! It must be quite serious, then; he wouldn't bother to tell his mother about every girl he dated, or...

Gina bit down on her lip, closing her eyes against a rush of anguish. Finish the sentence! she furiously told herself. Or slept with! Nick hadn't taken Colette to Luxembourg to discuss company finances with her. There could only be one reason why he asked her to go with him. They could have a few days together away from prying eyes and whispering tongues—and that was something he would not talk to his mother about!

When she felt able to go back to the sitting-room, she found Alessa standing by the huge plate-glass windows staring over the dark river at the lights of the night-time city.

'This is some view! I'd love to paint it. It reminds me of those Whistler paintings of the Thames at night...'

'Nocturnes, didn't he call them?'

'Yes, I think he did. I'm stunned that it still looks the way it did when he painted it, in spite of all the sky-scrapers and modern lighting.'

'It looks different in daylight, nowhere near as romantic!' Gina joined her and asked a question which had been on her mind ever since she met them in Heathrow. 'Why where you painting in Tuscany in the dead of winter? Isn't it very cold there at this time of year?'

'Yes, it is now, but I went there in summer, just for a month—and stayed on and on! I liked the people and the village I was living in, there was such a sense of continuity. Everything was old and lived in; the colours were amazing, faded terracotta and rose, umber and ochre— I kept seeing things to paint.'

'Are you going back there, when your mother returns to San Francisco?'

'I may do, but I haven't made plans.' Alessa shrugged. 'I never make plans, I like to let life surprise me.'

Gina considered her. 'You may look like your brother, but actually you're not like him at all, are you?'

'Is that a compliment, or an accusation?' Alessa was clearly unworried, whichever it was, and Gina smiled.

'I'm not sure, but Nick is always making plans, decisions, always looking ahead and manipulating the world around him—he's incapable of just letting life surprise him.'

'So it's a compliment! You don't approve of the way Nick tries to run everything he comes across!'

'No, I don't,' Gina said with a flare of defiance, her russet head lifting and her green eyes angrily bright.

Alessa grinned at her. 'No, neither do I, but he can't help it, he learnt it from our father, who was obsessed with controlling everything and everyone. I suppose he was afraid of what might happen if he didn't. A psychologist friend tells me it's fear that causes these obsessional neuroses, a terror of losing control of themselves as much as other people. Nick was one of the possessions my father felt he owned. He warped Nick. Luckily, as a mere girl I wasn't important, he mostly ignored me, and that warped me, too, I suppose. I knew my father didn't care a damn about me, so with me the reaction took a different form. I grew up angry and afraid of my own feelings. I guess that's why I never married. Every time I fall in love with some guy I start getting panic attacks and have to get away. They never understand.'

Gina gave her a startled look. Alessa's frankness was as hard to deal with as Nick's reticence.

'I don't suppose they would!' she said slowly. 'Have you tried explaining?'

'I'm never there long enough, and I never go back. My work takes up too much of my life, anyway. There isn't room for things like a husband or kids.'

'Don't you want a child?' Gina couldn't hide her own very different feelings, her voice husky with the longing she had felt for a long time.

Alessa watched her wryly. 'No, not really. You do, I suppose?'

Gina nodded, flushing. 'I always have. I was married very young, and although we wanted a baby we thought we had plenty of time for that, so we put it off...' She broke off, feeling the old grief again and Alessa gave her a sympathetic look.

'What happened?'

'He was killed,' Gina said starkly, and Alessa grimaced.

'That was tough luck. I'm sorry, Gina.'

'It was all a long time ago, I still miss him, but it doesn't hurt the way it did once. It's just a gentle regret now.' Gina turned back into the room to change the subject and Alessa followed, talking casually, as if to smooth the moment over.

'Well, I'm not the maternal type. Now, Nick wants kids. I'm amazed he's never married and had some, but he's such a perfectionist he never seems to find exactly the right girl.' She laughed shortly. 'Or maybe, like me, he gets panic attacks if he starts falling in love, and runs away.'

'I can't imagine Nick having panic attacks!' said Gina bitterly, and Alessa gave her a shrewd, searching look, but before she could ask any more questions there was a long ring on the doorbell and Gina tensed. 'That's probably him now! I'd better let him in before he wakes your mother up!'

Nick was leaning on the door frame when she opened the door, his coat collar up around his hard face, his black hair tousled by the winter wind. Moodily, he surveyed her from head to foot, through eyes that glinted behind his black lashes like dark water among reeds.

'I had a message to say that my mother was with you,' he muttered, and she could see he didn't intend to offer her any apologies for the way he'd behaved last time they met. On the contrary, Nick had come back sulky and accusing, as if he had convinced himself it was she who had behaved badly.

CHAPTER FIVE

'YES, so you might as well come in,' Gina said, making sure her tone was very cool and distinctly unwelcoming, in case he thought she had forgotten the way he had humiliated her at Hazel's party. 'Your mother is lying down at the moment, in my spare bedroom, but your sister is in the sitting-room.'

He stopped dead, as he walked past her, gave her a narrow-eyed look. 'Sister?'

'Alessa.'

'Well, I realised that,' he said impatiently, as if she was being very stupid. 'I knew my mother had been staying with her, I was just surprised to hear Alessa had come to London too.'

'I got the impression she thought your mother shouldn't travel alone, and I must say Mrs Caspian looked very tired. That's why she's lying down now.'

'She isn't very strong; travelling tires her,' Nick agreed in an absent tone. 'I can't understand why she didn't wait for me to get back to London so that I could make the arrangements for her trip. She should have stayed in Tuscany until I sent the jet to get her the way I always do, then she could lie down during the journey. And where is Mrs Grant? My mother never goes anywhere without her. That's the main part of her job—to take care of my mother—so where the hell is she?'

Gina had no answers for him, since neither Mrs Caspian nor her daughter had so much as mentioned Mrs Grant. So she just shrugged, closing the front door, while Nick walked on into the sitting-room. She heard him say, 'Alessa, what are you doing here? And what on earth does Mama think she's playing at?'

Gina didn't wait to hear Alessa's answer; she turned and walked away, to the kitchen to deal with the glasses, cups and saucers and plates that had been used a little earlier by Mrs Caspian and her daughter. She washed the glasses by hand, but stacked everything else in the dishwasher. The machine was always put on each morning, and later emptied, and the dishes put away by the woman who cleaned her apartment.

She made some coffee at the same time and when she felt she had given Nick and his sister enough time alone she carried a tray through to them, hearing Alessa's cool voice as she approached the sitting-room door.

'You may say she was over-reacting, but when you talked to her about this Colette Tse it upset her. She'd thought...well, for some reason, she had decided it would be Gina...'

Gina felt a stab of pain and went pale. She didn't want to hear Nick's answer to that, so to make sure they knew she was coming, she deliberately let her tray knock loudly against the door before she pushed it open.

They both fell silent. Alessa gave her a quick, faintly embarrassed smile, obviously wondering how much she had heard, and Nick turned those moody eyes on her, his mouth taut.

She put the tray down on a table. 'Coffee—will you both have some?'

'No, thanks,' he said ungraciously, scowling. She felt like smacking him, and maybe that was his trouble. He hadn't been smacked often enough when he was a child.

Alessa gave him a dry glance, as if she thought so too. Then she smiled at Gina, her face apologetic. 'You're very hospitable, Gina; would you let me take a rain-check on that offer? Now Nick is here we could move our cases into his apartment, and I can unpack for my mother before she wakes up. She does so hate that part of travelling, being in transit, not settled. She says it makes her feel like a refugee with her life in parcels. If she finds her room ready, her clothes in the wardrobes and drawers, the bed turned down, her photograph frames put out, her little travelling clock...all the personal little items she takes with her everywhere...she'll feel more secure.'

'Of course, I understand,' Gina said warmly. 'And if you need any help, don't hesitate to ask...'

'Thank you, you've been a tower of strength already. I really can't thank you enough for everything you've done.'

'It was a pleasure.'

'Where are the cases?' muttered Nick, still looking sullen.

Pretending not to notice his expression, Gina showed him where the company chauffeur had put them. Nick and Alessa began moving them, refusing her offer of help. Gina watched them cross to Nick's apartment, went back into the sitting-room, poured herself some coffee and sat down on the couch in front of the electric fire with it.

A few minutes later Nick came back, alone. 'Alessa is unpacking for my mother,' he said, and sat down beside her on the couch.

Gina's nerves thudded in panic. She leapt up, trembling. 'Will you have that coffee now?'

He threw himself back, his long, lean body relaxing against the cushions, his eyes glinting derisively behind their dark lashes.

'You're very jumpy tonight. Scared of being alone with me, Gina?'

She lifted her chin angrily. 'Don't kid yourself. If I have to, I can take you on, even if I have to beat you over the head with that lamp there!'

He laughed shortly. 'I believe you would!'

'You'd better believe it!' she nodded at him, her green eyes spitting defiance. 'And, anyway, I'm sure you wouldn't want to risk having me scream the place down with your mother just a couple of rooms away!'

Nick's eyes were glittering furiously by now. 'Oh, pour my coffee before I lose my temper with you!'

'You mean you haven't lost it already?' she taunted, but she poured the coffee and handed him a cup, then took her own over to a chair on the other side of the hearth.

Nick took a sip, sighed. 'I have to say, you make very good coffee.' His eyes half-closed, his black lashes against his cheek, he gave her a curling little smile and Gina felt her breathing quicken, a pulse start beating in her throat. If only he weren't so attractive! Every time she saw him she felt a strange, piercing ache deep inside; a fire, a sweetness, which was both pain and pleasure. He drew her, like a magnet, making her shudder with an erotic longing to touch him, be close to him. When he wasn't with her, she daydreamed about him, or was with him in her sleep. He haunted, obsessed her. Gina would never have believed herself to be so weak, and she despised herself for it.

'So,' Nick said lazily, stretching like a sleepy cat, 'tell me what's been going on while my back was turned!'

Her nerves tightened. 'You've been getting your reports every day, haven't you?'

She knew he had because she was responsible for putting together a daily report for him and making sure he got it, wherever he was in the world. That was how Nick kept his finger on the pulse of all his separate national companies; they each had to file a report with his office. He didn't necessarily read every one, but an abbreviated round-up of all the reports was made up every day, by one of his senior secretaries, and Nick read that.

'The official picture, yes,' he drawled. 'But what has been happening unofficially? How are you getting on with Sophie, for instance?'

'Fine,' she said, relaxing. 'I knew I liked her; that was why I suggested her to you.'

'Yes,' he said in a slow, thoughtful way, his eyes skimming over her face. 'You chose her, I'd forgotten.'

'I suggested her,' agreed Gina.

He was frowning again. 'OK, let's rephrase it...you wanted her to take Hazel's place, and she did. You got your own way. In fact, you get your own way more and more these days, don't you? You run the *Sentinel* when I'm not there, and even when I am I find myself having to do things your way!'

She was incredulous. 'Are you being funny?'

'Do I look as if I am?' he snarled, scowling, not laughing.

'You look as if you're in a temper again,' Gina snapped back at him. 'These days you usually are! Well, I'm sick of you and your moods.'

She got up and put her empty coffee-cup on the tray, intending to walk out of the room with it, but Nick had got up, too. He caught her shoulders and swung her round towards him.

Startled, Gina shot a look up at him; his face was grim, his grey eyes penetrating as they searched her face.

'Do you think I don't realise you're up to something, Gina?' he bit out, and the colour drained from her face.

'Wha-what do you mean?' she stammered.

Nick shook her fiercely, looming over her in a threatening way, making her very nervous. 'I have a sixth sense where conspiracy is concerned. I know something is wrong in London. All my instincts tell me so, and they also tell me that whatever is going on is centred around you!'

'Y-you're paranoid!' Gina stammered, struggling to get away from him and failing.

His face tightened. 'Yes, maybe I am, where you're concerned,' he said in a low, hoarse voice, staring down at her, and Gina's green eyes widened and darkened as he gazed into them. 'And I have good reason to be, haven't I?'

'That's crazy!' she protested and he laughed bitterly.

'Then you've made me crazy. I don't know what I'm doing, what I think, what I want...sometimes I feel I'm losing my grip on my entire business, all because of you. If this weren't the twentieth century, and I weren't an educated man, I'd say you'd put a spell on me!'

She was so wound up herself that she began to laugh, a little hysterically.

Nick turned dark red and glowered at her, his face clenched in temper.

'Don't laugh at me, you little witch!' His fingers dug into her shoulders, dragged her closer. Their bodies touched and she felt a white-hot flare of need go through her.

'Stop it!' she groaned, beginning to shake. 'Let go of me, or I'll...I'll make you wish you had...'

He didn't even seem to hear her. She felt his arm across her back, rigid as an iron bar, holding her; his head blotted out the light, his eyes staring down at her, glittering with menace.

'Don't threaten me, Gina,' he muttered.

She felt her knees giving, she could scarcely breathe, her ears thundering with hypertension. Nick's eyes slowly moved their gaze downwards until he was staring at her parted, quivering mouth.

'What will you do to me, anyway? Turn me into a toad?' And he laughed huskily at his own joke. Gina wasn't so amused.

'I'm too late, you've been one for years!' she furiously told him, and saw the laughter leave his eyes.

'You really are asking for it, aren't you?' he bit out, and a second later his mouth closed over hers. She gasped at the force of that kiss, driving her head back, his lips hot and urgent. She was almost suffocating, she couldn't breathe; the feel of his body pressed against her made her dizzy as if she might be going to faint. Her eyes closed weakly and she had to lean on him to stay on her feet.

'Oh, Gina, Gina,' Nick whispered a few moments later, his face buried in her neck, his lips caressing her cool, pale skin. 'I want you so badly, and you want me.'

She wordlessly shook her head, shuddering, but how could she hope to convince him when her own body betrayed her every time he touched her?

'Yes, you know you do,' he impatiently insisted. 'You couldn't kiss me like that if you didn't.'

She closed her eyes again. Oh, God, it was true; why couldn't she hide it from him?

He held her, his cheek against her hair, one hand running caressingly up and down her spine, stroking her neck. 'Gina, Gina... can't we stop fighting each other? Can't you put the past behind you, forget the Tyrrells and your husband...?'

She winced at the reminder of James, knowing she had never loved him with this agonising intensity. Theirs had been a first love, young and sweet, with no real depth. They had been strangers to such pain. Her green eyes opened, dark with a sense of betrayal, and Nick stared down into them broodingly, his face jealous as he tried to read her thoughts in them.

'You can't go on forever living in their shadow, it isn't healthy!' he muttered harshly. 'It's a sin against life. Sooner or later you've got to face it—they're dead, and we aren't! We still have our lives in front of us. What's the point of fighting old battles, keeping old grudges alive? I'll admit I haven't behaved too well in the past, I don't pretend to be perfect, but at least I learn from my mistakes. Why can't you? We're wasting time making war when we could be making love——'

Angrily Gina gave him a push so violent that it sent him reeling backwards, almost hitting the wall.

'How many times do I have to tell you? If you want a woman, find one somewhere else!' she hissed at him. 'I'm not available! I work for you at the *Sentinel*. I'm not paid to jump into your bed whenever you snap your fingers!'

Nick straightened, his face white with rage, looking as if he was tempted to hit her back, and Gina was so furious that her green eyes dared him to! She would almost have welcomed the violence, her feelings were so out of hand.

'I loved my husband, and his grandfather,' she threw at him, as if the words were hand grenades. 'I don't want to forget them or abandon everything they believed in!'

'I didn't ask you to——'

'Oh, yes, you did! You want me to let you do as you like with their newspaper, without daring to say a word of protest! Well, I can't stop you yet, much as I'd love to, but while there's breath in my body I'll go on protesting! You're destroying a great newspaper. For the moment you may control the *Sentinel* but one day that could change—anything is possible! And then I hope I'll see the paper return to the standards the Tyrrells stood for.'

There was a long silence, while he stared narrowly at her. 'Is that what you're plotting, Gina?' he asked at last, his voice derisive. 'You dream of getting me out of the *Sentinel* and taking control yourself, do you? Well, enjoy your daydreams, because that's all they are. It will never happen. You haven't got a snowball's chance in hell of dislodging me from my position. I control that newspaper because I have money behind me, and when the chips are down the men with the financial backing always win. You have just as many shares, but you don't have any other large capital backing, and to get it you would have to mortgage or sell some of your shares.

You can't beat me, Gina. You only have one option—to join me.'

'In your bed?' she sneered, her face bitter. 'That's all you think a woman is good for, isn't it?'

He laughed, cold mockery in his eyes. 'Oh, I'm just an old-fashioned boy at heart!'

'Heart?' she repeated contemptuously. 'Don't talk about hearts, Nick. What would you know about them? You haven't got one! Or you wouldn't still think you had a chance of talking me round after the way you humiliated me at Hazel's party!'

His face changed; he grimaced. 'Oh, that,' he said on a sound like a groan. 'Yes...' Then he gave her a sideways look, his lashes flickering over his eyes, a coaxing little smile tugging at his mouth. 'Gina, I'm sorry... I know I behaved badly...'

Did he really expect her to be taken in by that naughty-boy look? she thought cynically, watching him with cold eyes.

Nick went on softly, 'My only excuse is that I was angry and upset and I wanted to hit out at you, hurt you the way you hurt me, when you refused to go home with me for Christmas.'

Unmoved, she retorted, 'At least I didn't insult you in public!'

'No, that was unforgivable of me,' he said in soulful tones, still looking at her through his lashes and trying to look appealing.

'But you expect to be forgiven!'

He gave a long sigh, looked at her with reproach, as if she was being unreasonable. 'I'm just trying to explain...'

She stared stonily back.

After a little silence he abandoned the little-boy look and said flatly, 'OK. Look, Gina, I'd told my mother you'd be there, I'd brought you Christmas presents, I'd planned it all. I can't remember when I last looked forward to a Christmas that much. Maybe never. I didn't have very good Christmases when I was a child. Some of them were pretty grim affairs. I would get expensive presents, huge Christmas trees...we used to spend some of them in Switzerland, so I'd go skiing and we would have picnics in the snow. But it was never a real family Christmas.'

His eyes were bleak as they stared over her head, as if at a vision she could not see. Gina watched him, so moved she could have cried. Nick was a very rich man, certainly one of the wealthiest men in Europe; but all his money could not buy him the happy childhood he had never known. More and more she realised how that childhood had marked him, made him the man he was today.

He frowned, shrugging away his memories, and said huskily, 'I wanted to make last Christmas a real family Christmas, my mother, my sister Lilith and her husband and children, Alessa, and you and me. I knew you had no family, I thought you'd enjoy it.' His mouth turned down at the corners in a sulky movement. 'But you turned me down...'

Gina was silent, staring at him. Sometimes he baffled her. On the surface he was a tough, hard-bitten businessman, with no weak points, no softer feelings, but under that hid a sulky, moody boy who couldn't bear to be rejected or disappointed.

The way he hit back was not so childish, however. She frowned at him. 'Is that why you took Colette Tse to Luxembourg with you?'

Nick gave her a startled look. 'What?'

'Did you think I wouldn't find out?' she asked bitterly, seeing admission in his face. 'The whole of Barbary Wharf knows! They're all talking about it—even your mother asked me about her, whether she was pretty, what she was like...so if you hoped to keep your affair with Colette a secret you can forget it!'

'Can I?' he said slowly, oddly, his eyes lowered, his mouth twitching slightly, as if he was trying not to smile, and that suggestion of amusement made Gina even angrier.

'But you didn't want to keep it a secret, did you?' she jealously accused. 'You flaunted it deliberately. I wouldn't have an affair with you, so you wanted to show me you only had to snap your fingers to get someone else. Shrewd of you to hit on Colette; she's very ambitious, she wouldn't hesitate, whatever you asked her to do, if it meant promotion!'

'Miaow! I've never noticed before how feline your big green eyes are!' Nick mocked and Gina's colour flared.

'Just get out of my flat, will you?' she shouted and he looked quickly at the door.

'Ssh...keep your voice down, you'll wake my mother.'

'If you don't want her upset, you'd better go before I start throwing things!' threatened Gina and he gave her a wry look.

'I believe you would.' Then his eyes gleamed. 'What a passionate creature you are, Gina! As I remember vividly...'

She was scarlet at the reminiscent tone, knowing he was talking about the one time they had slept together. 'Shut up!'

'At least now I know what I'm missing, and the memory is unforgettable,' Nick mocked.

'It will never happen again!' Gina hoarsely muttered, hating him for that smile, the taunting amusement in his grey eyes.

'Don't bet on it!' Nick said softly, and Gina felt her throat tighten with alarm.

Then he looked at his watch, and shrugged. 'Well, I'd better go and see how Alessa is coping with the unpacking. My mother usually travels everywhere with Mrs Grant to take care of her, but while they were in Italy Mrs Grant suddenly had an urgent call from her sister, who had been taken seriously ill, and flew off back to the States. She suggested that my mother should go too, but Mama preferred to stay on with Alessa. Heaven only knows if or when Mrs Grant will come back, or what Mama will do without her. While she is in London I'll have to find her a temporary companion-secretary.' He gave Gina an uncertain glance. 'I suppose you wouldn't take on the job of finding someone for her? I'd leave it to Sophie, but she doesn't know my mother, she wouldn't have a clue how to pick somebody. It can be time-consuming, interviewing people, and I have a hell of a lot on my plate at the moment, but I must find the right sort of person.'

'Won't your mother want to make the choice?'

'If you narrow it down to two or three people, Mama can decide which she prefers,' he agreed. 'But she isn't up to interviewing dozens of applicants. Would you, Gina? I know I can trust you to find the right person, you know my mother and what she likes.'

'I like your mother,' Gina said coolly. 'Yes, I'll find her someone I think she'll like.'

'Thank you.'

Nick began to walk to the door, but as he opened it so his mother's voice said sleepily from the other end of the apartment. 'Nick? Is that you?'

He turned, smiling, his grey eyes warmly lit. 'Yes, Mama—did we wake you up? I'm sorry, you must be so tired.'

She came towards them slowly and embraced him. 'No, dear, I've had a nap, and I feel quite rested now. I was just waking up when I thought I heard your voice.'

He kissed her on both cheeks, then straightened and looked searchingly into her face. 'Was the journey very tiring? Why on earth didn't you let me know you were coming to London right away, then I could have sent my jet for you?'

'I knew you were using it today,' she said, her voice very Spanish on some words, the ghost of an 'h' appearing and disappearing before some vowels. 'And anyway, it was such a short trip from Milan to London, I flew first class and the girls on the plane were wonderful, they fussed over me as if I was their own mother. It wasn't so very tiring. I'm always tired after a flight, even on your jet.' She turned to smile at Gina, patting her arm. 'And Gina met me and brought me here, and gave me somewhere nice and quiet to lie down! She has been an angel. So don't fuss, Nick, I'm stronger than you think.'

He laughed and put his arm around her shoulders, turning her towards the front door. 'Alessa has done your unpacking. Your room is ready for you—come and see my apartment.'

Mrs Caspian leaned over to kiss Gina's cheek. 'Thank you for looking after me so well, Gina. I hope I'm going to see a lot more of you while I'm in London. Nick will arrange it, won't you, Nick? I'm certainly not spending all my free time with this Colette Tse.'

Gina stiffened, her eyes shooting from Mrs Caspian to Nick, but his face was unrevealing, his eyes hooded, his features bland.

'I'll arrange everything,' he said. 'Come along, Mama, we've taken up too much of Gina's time already this evening.'

'Oh, of course,' his mother said hastily, letting him steer her away. 'Goodnight, Gina. I'll see you again soon.'

'Goodnight,' said Gina quietly as the front door closed behind them. She slowly walked back into her sitting-room, her mind feverish. Nick kept pursuing her, making love to her, flirting with her, but he never asked her to marry him. Was he playing the same game with Colette? Or was their relationship more serious? Why else was his mother here, in London, and talking of spending time with Colette?

CHAPTER SIX

A FEW days later, Gina arrived at the office a little earlier than usual, expecting to find herself alone until Sophie got there at nine, but as soon as she opened her door Nick shot out of his own office, his face dark with rage.

'Did you know they were going to pull the plug on the graveyard shift?'

'What?' She was too taken aback to register the accusation for a moment.

Nick hadn't waited for her to think about it. His voice raw, he said, 'Do you know how many copies we lost? Almost the entire last edition. 'The north-west of England didn't get their *Sentinel* this morning. That only has to happen a few times a month for us to start bleeding to death financially. I thought we'd put that sort of craziness behind us. What the hell is going on down there?'

'I don't even know what you're talking about, Nick!' Gina slowly took off her coat and hung it up, frowning at him. 'Give me a chance to get inside the door before you start bellowing at me, would you? It's too early in the morning for this sort of commotion, and I need a cup of strong coffee.'

She turned her back on Nick, went over to her desk and rang the large office across the corridor where much of the daily routine work was done. A cheerful voice answered with a gabbled routine response.

'Mr Caspian's office, Secretarial, Gillian Hawkins speaking, can I help you?'

'Gillian, this is Mrs Tyrrell, would you make some coffee and bring it through to my office? Two cups.'

'Biscuits, Mrs Tyrrell?'

'No, thanks, just coffee.'

Feeling calmer, Gina sat down behind her desk and looked up at Nick. 'Now, would you start again at the beginning and this time tell me exactly what went wrong last night?'

He surveyed her with hostile eyes. 'You have no idea?' The question was sarcastic, making it clear he didn't believe her.

Gina gave him a furious stare. 'None whatever! What are you accusing me of? Conspiring with the men now? You really are becoming paranoid.'

He smiled tightly. 'Am I? I wonder. Last night the printing works came to a halt. I called in on my way home from a big reception at the Guildhall, at around midnight, and found utter chaos down there. The last run had stopped about five minutes after it started. An electrical fault, they hurriedly said, when I walked in and found most of them just standing about smoking and chatting among themselves. Everything just shut down, without warning, they said. So what about all those safety factors built into the process, the back-ups that should have been available to take over? I asked them. Ah, well, apparently they came into operation and then almost immediately they blew too!' His eyes were savage. 'Coincidence, wasn't it? How come both systems went? I asked them. The circuits on the back-up must have been overloaded, they told me—but when I asked them how the hell the back-up circuits could be overloaded by taking over, when it was designed for just that purpose, they didn't have any answers, just mumbled and shifted their feet.'

Gina bit her lip, frowning. 'How long did the problem last? It has been put right now, I suppose?'

He shook his head. 'We had to call in the firm who installed the machinery, and their men didn't arrive until eight o'clock this morning. They were busy elsewhere;

they could only do one job at a time, I was told. I had to send the late-shift men home. I didn't notice any of them dragging his feet or offering to stay on in case the "fault" cleared up in the same mysterious way it appeared. We just had to abandon the last edition and wipe those copies off the slate.'

'But what makes you think the fault wasn't just bad luck?' protested Gina and he laughed curtly.

'My instinct.'

She looked at him with unsmiling derision. 'The same "instinct" that tells you I'm always plotting against you?'

'Well, aren't you?' he asked pointedly, and she wished she could deny it outright, but how could she when it was true?

Not quite meeting his eyes, she tried to make a joke of it. 'Sure I am!' Then quickly went on, 'But even if there was some sabotage last night, will you be able to prove it?'

'If there's any evidence of sabotage Roboprint's men will find it. They're the experts; those machines will be stripped and examined inch by inch until we know for sure what really happened.' He frowned at her. 'You know where you are if men go on open strike, but I won't put up with dirty tricks masquerading as accidents. What happened last night was deliberate, and I want to know who's behind it, before it happens again!'

There was a tap on the door, and Gillian Hawkins came in, carrying a tray on which stood a pot of coffee and two cups and saucers, a sugar bowl, and a jug of skimmed milk.

A small, fresh-faced girl of around eighteen, with round blue eyes and curly brown hair, she gave Nick a shy look, apologising hurriedly. 'We only have skimmed milk, in the office, sir.' Then giggled nervously. 'We're all on diets.'

'You don't need to diet! Your figure is perfect as it is!' he said, giving her that knock-them-down smile he

used when he wanted to charm a woman. Gina watched
him with cynicism. The girl was big-eyed with ador-
ation. It was obvious that she regarded Nick as a
fabulous creature, as out of her reach as a film star. She
was quivering from head to foot as she poured Nick's
coffee. She was new this month and had probably never
come into contact with him before, only seen him walking
past, maybe, or simply heard about him.

'Do you want milk, sir?' she asked now, jug poised.

'No, I take it black,' he said. 'You're new, aren't you?
What's your name?'

'Gillian,' she said breathlessly, handing him his cup.

'Well, thank you, Gillian,' Nick said, smiling.

She poured Gina her coffee and reluctantly left. Nick
watched her go, amused, his mouth indulgent.

'Pretty kid!'

Gina gave him a dry look. 'They call it cradle-
snatching, you know.'

He laughed, grey eyes glinting. 'You sound cross,
Gina. Why's that?'

The phone rang and he picked it up automatically
before she could move. 'Hello? Oh. No, Guy, she isn't
here yet. Ring back later. While we're talking, have we
heard any more from the Bolton brothers' solicitor? No,
we're not settling out of court. I know their game—
blackmail under another name. Nobody blackmails me.'

Gina sipped her black coffee, her brow pleated. As
Nick said, 'I'll see you at the afternoon conference,' and
hung up, she gave him a worried look.

'The Bolton brothers? That's the East End Mafia
story, isn't it? Are they still threatening you?'

'They don't bother me,' said Nick with an offhand
shrug, then in dry tones, 'Not even as much as you do!
Look, as the printing workers think you're so wonderful, maybe you can talk some sense into them, and
get them to stop making trouble before they all find
themselves out of jobs!'

Ever since she had defended the printing workers last year Nick had insisted on blaming her for everything that happened in the printing works, but she was not taking responsibility for something that was most probably an accident.

'I don't believe the men would deliberately sabotage the machinery! It would soon show up if they had interfered with it, and they wouldn't risk their jobs with a stupid trick like that.'

'We'll see,' said Nick grimly, taking his coffee over to the window and staring out with his back to her.

Gina drank some of her own coffee, absent-mindedly picking up a folder that had been delivered that morning and lay in her in-tray. It contained the sales and advertising figures for the previous month; she flicked the folder open and ran her eye over the columns.

After a moment, she stiffened, turning her sharp green gaze on Nick. 'I suppose you've seen these?'

He swung round and gave the folder a glance. 'The monthly figures? Yes, of course.'

'Circulation up almost one per cent!' Gina exclaimed incredulously, and he gave her a sardonic smile.

'Were you hoping for a further drop?'

'That was the projection we had, for the circulation to go on falling for the present!' she said evasively, looking away. Nick had a mysterious ability to make shrewd guesses, even when he didn't realise quite what he was saying. It was vital to the success of Sir Dermot's plans for the circulation figures to stay down. It had been the fall in revenue from sales and advertising over the previous few months which had made the rest of the board swing round towards Nick's enemies. If it looked as if he was back on a winning streak their fair-weather friends would rush back to support his side and wreck all hope of voting him out of power.

'Well, the chart analysts were wrong. It looks as if we've turned the corner, although of course you can never be sure about anything.' His eyes were coldly personal. 'Or anyone,' he added, his mouth twisting.

Gina changed the subject. 'Are Alessa and your mother enjoying their visit?'

'My mother doesn't enjoy London very much, especially in winter. She's homesick for San Francisco.'

'I can't say I blame her. She has such a lovely home. If it was mine I'd never leave it.'

'She doesn't, very often. The only reason she went to Italy was because my sister seemed to have taken root there and Mama wanted to find out what she was up to.'

Gina laughed. 'And what was she up to?'

'Painting!' said Nick drily. 'Alessa doesn't seem to have a love life at the moment.'

Gina remembered what Alessa had said about falling in love and then getting a panic attack and running away. Had Alessa ever told Nick about her emotional hang-ups?

'By the way,' he said offhandedly, 'I booked a box at the theatre tomorrow night for Mama and Alessa to see the new musical version of *Alice in Wonderland* and she wondered if you would join them.'

'That's very kind of her. I've been dying to see it but I hadn't got around to it,' Gina said slowly, trying to think. Was he going to be there? And what if he brought Colette? It was common knowledge around the paper that he and Colette had been seen leaving together several evenings that week, and as she got out of the lift in the apartment block one evening at around eleven after having dinner with Roz and Daniel in their flat Gina had heard Colette's voice from Nick's apartment. She didn't know if Colette had spent the night there, or what Mrs Caspian thought of it if she had—but Gina didn't think she could face spending an entire evening in their company, having to watch them together, see for herself what everyone was talking about.

Nick was watching her fixedly; the insistent probe of the hard grey eyes making her nervous. 'Well?' he snapped impatiently. 'Will you or won't you?'

'Don't snarl at me!'

'I wasn't snarling!' he snarled, his face moody. 'I just wish I understood what went on inside your head. You baffle me. You always seem to like my mother, and I know she's become very fond of you—so why do you always seem reluctant to spend any time with her? You wouldn't spend Christmas with her, you're obviously not jumping at the invitation to go to the theatre——'

'I'm not reluctant to see her!' she protested, horrified by the accusation. She would hate it if he said something along those lines to his mother; Gina wouldn't hurt Mrs Caspian's feelings for worlds! 'I think your mother is a darling, and I find it easy to talk to her.'

'Then why are you hesitating?'

She met his eyes defiantly. 'Are you going to be there?'

His mouth set in a straight line; he stared down at her, scowling. Through his teeth he bit out words as if he hated their taste. 'I see. It's me you don't want to spend time with, is it? It must be tough for you here, every day, having to share an office with me! Maybe you'd better resign and get a job somewhere else!'

Very flushed, she retorted furiously, 'If anyone should leave, it's you, not me!'

He laughed without amusement. 'Oh, you'd love that, wouldn't you? Now tell me I'm suffering from paranoia!'

'I don't deny I want to see you walking out of the *Sentinel* for good!'

'Well, too bad. I am not going anywhere.' He gave her a tight, angry smile. 'Now, do I tell my mother yes or no?'

She was angry enough herself by then to snap, 'Yes!' deciding that she wasn't going to be intimidated by the risk of finding Colette one of the party. Let them flirt; why should she care?

Nick's mouth twisted coldly. 'Sure you'll be able to stand my company for an evening?'

'I'll grit my teeth!'

His eyes hardened. 'You are the most——' He broke off, taking a long, deep breath. Then he said levelly, 'We'll be going straight from work to have a little light pre-theatre dinner at the Savoy; it's only just across the Strand from the theatre.' Turning on his heel as he said the last word, he walked off without waiting for her to respond and Gina stared after him, feeling chill and depressed. Why did they always end up quarrelling like cat and dog?

But of course she knew why—there was no point in pretending she didn't, except that she preferred not to face the facts. She and Nick were constantly in emotional confrontation, torn between love and hate, see-sawing back and forth from minute to minute; how could they ever achieve any sort of truce? There was no middle way for them. They either fought, or made love, and Gina refused to let him sweet-talk her into bed again. Her self-respect wouldn't stand it.

Sophie arrived five minutes later, breathless and flushed with windswept hair. 'Sorry, there was some sort of accident on the Underground, my train was stuck in a tunnel for twenty minutes and then we had to get out a station too soon, and I couldn't get on a bus, I had to walk the rest of the way.'

'London gets worse every day,' Gina sympathised. 'It's being strangled! Too much traffic, too many people. If somebody doesn't do something soon, this city won't be worth living in!'

'I sometimes envy my Uncle Theo—he lives somewhere else, at least in his head,' Sophie said, hanging up her coat and giving her reflection a groaning stare before getting out a brush and hurriedly doing something to her hair.

'Where does he think he lives?' asked Gina, intrigued.

'Budapest. Even on a mild day here in winter he goes out wearing a fur hat, fur gloves, a thick overcoat and boots. In Budapest winter is much colder than it usually is here, so he's always surprised if it isn't snowing when he goes out.'

Gina laughed. 'I love your family—you're so lucky, having them. I haven't got as much as an aunt, let alone an uncle like yours.'

'Well, I love them, too, but they can drive me crazy,' said Sophie. 'You must get married again, and make sure you pick someone with a big family!'

'I'll bear the advice in mind,' said Gina with wry amusement. 'This coffee is still hot; have a cup before you start work.'

She had lunch with Roz Amery at Pierre's; they had a standing arrangement to meet for lunch whenever Roz was in London, which these days was not too often. Over a winter meal of vegetable broth followed by lightly curried prawns and banana, they talked about a whole range of subjects—politics, a French film Roz had seen in Paris a few days earlier, last night's breakdown in the printing works and Nick's reaction to it.

'He's convinced it was deliberate sabotage!' said Gina, sipping some mineral water flavoured with lime.

'And was it?' Roz cynically asked, eyeing her across the table with raised brows.

'Heaven knows. I certainly don't! And don't look at me like that, Roz. Nick may believe I'm conspiring with all his enemies behind his back, but you surely don't think that?'

Roz made a face. 'Maybe not *all* his enemies!'

Gina met her eyes and groaned. 'Oh, Roz, I'm in such a muddle. I can't make up my mind how I feel about him, I can't make up my mind what to do...'

With wry sympathy Roz said, 'I did warn you!'

'Don't keep saying that!'

'Sorry! I can't help it. I can't believe you would be so stupid as to let yourself care too much for someone like Nick Caspian. He's been chased by dozens of other women, you know, some pretty gorgeous ones, too; and rich, from very classy backgrounds. Sometimes he let them think they'd caught him.' Roz gave her a wry smile. 'For a while. Then when he was tired of them he played Houdini and vanished into thin air. Several times it was rumoured he was going to get married; once, I believe, he actually got engaged, years ago, but nothing came of that, either. Men like Nick Caspian have so much to offer that they get very picky. They want nothing less than perfection, and, of course, that isn't so easy to find, and as the years go by their chances of finding it grow less and less. I don't suppose he will ever get married now, or else he'll suddenly marry some young girl, when he's desperate enough, just to have children.'

Gina shivered, close to tears. 'Don't.'

Roz gave a Gallic shrug. 'OK, don't face facts.'

'That's what I'm doing. When I remember the way the *Sentinel* used to be and look at today's paper, I feel sick. And yet there's no denying it sells more copies than the Tyrrells ever did. People seem to prefer his style of journalism.' Gina rubbed her forehead, sighing. 'Oh, I don't know what to think...'

The waiter came and removed their plates, and offered them the dessert card, but they said they would just take coffee. He brought it immediately, in a small silver pot, and poured them each a cup, which they drank black and without sugar.

When they were alone again, Roz sipped, smiled. 'Their coffee really is good, you know, although I can't get Daniel to admit it.'

She was changing the subject and Gina seized on it gratefully. 'Have you fixed your wedding date yet?'

'Easter,' said Roz. 'It is going to be a huge affair. Daniel has simply hundreds of relatives scattered across

France and Quebec Province. They won't all come, but
he'll have far more relatives on his side than I will.'

'Where will you have your honeymoon?'

'Daniel won't tell me. It's a surprise; all he'll say is
that it's somewhere I haven't been.'

Gina laughed. 'That doesn't leave much scope for the
imagination—you must have been practically everywhere by now, in your roving reporter days.'

Roz's expression grew rueful, half nostalgic. 'Yes, I
suppose I have seen most parts of the globe. I'll be quite
relieved to settle down in Paris for good when my father
gives up the job.'

'I thought you weren't going to take it?'

'I changed my mind.'

Startled, Gina gave her a searching look. 'How does
Daniel feel about that?'

'We've discussed it ever since Nick made me the offer.
I saw how Hazel felt about living apart from Piet while
he was in Holland and she was here. I didn't think it
would work, but Daniel talked me into accepting. After
all, we're used to being apart, and he'll be quite relieved
to have me permanently living somewhere as civilised as
Paris instead of roving around the world to trouble spots
where I could always wind up getting shot or blown up.
At least in Paris the worst I'll have to fear is being mown
down trying to cross the Etoile at lunchtime! Of course,
we'll be separated for five days a week, but we'll only
be a couple of hours apart, we can see each other often,
and I may only stay in Paris for a year or so. Daniel and
I are considering going back to Montreal to live. We
rather like the idea of bringing up a family there, rather
than back here in Europe.'

Gina gave her a stricken look. 'I'd never see you!'

Roz sighed. 'Well, not very often, I know, and I'll
miss you, too, but it will be a while before all this
happens, don't look so gloomy.'

'How can I help it?' wailed Gina. 'Hazel has gone, and now you're planning to move to the other side of the world...everything is changing, Roz. Just over a year ago, the *Sentinel* was run by Sir George and we were still in Fleet Street, and Hazel hadn't met Piet, and you weren't engaged to Daniel, and I barely knew the name Nick Caspian!'

'That's life, though, isn't it?' Roz said quite gently. 'The world changes every day, and so do we. Don't they say that every seven years every cell in your body is different? So I'm looking at you now and the Gina I see is not the same physical Gina I knew seven years ago. You look the same on the outside, but inside you've been totally replaced, cell by cell.'

'That is spooky!' Gina shuddered. 'You made that up!'

'Cross my heart, I didn't.'

'Seven years ago James was still alive.' Gina's face had turned pale, her green eyes haunted. 'I never thought I'd ever fall in love again, you know, after he died.' She broke off, her lips quivering. 'Don't you find it terrifying, Roz? The way life just rolls on over you, like a great tidal wave. It lifts you up and carries you on somewhere else and you don't have a chance of fighting it. You often don't even understand what's happening to you. One minute you're standing there with someone you love, or a friend, feeling fine, thinking your life is settled forever—and the next life has torn away everything familiar, wrecked your happiness...left you stranded and alone.'

Roz watched her with concern, frowning. 'You are having a bad time, aren't you? Look, have dinner with me and Daniel tonight—it won't be cordon bleu, I was planing spaghetti, but we can talk, and try to cheer you up!'

'I'd love to, Roz, but I'm going to see the new *Alice in Wonderland* musical tonight.' Gina paused, adding drily, 'With Nick and his mother and sister.'

Roz lifted her brows. 'Oh, are you? Well, with his mother around you should be safe enough.'

Gina remembered the dry comment later that evening when she and Nick were left alone in the office by Sophie's departure dead on six. As soon as the office door closed behind her the tension between the two of them grew until it filled the room, making Gina's ears buzz with hypertension and her pulses beat like jungle drums.

'What time are we meeting your mother and Alessa?' she asked Nick huskily.

'Six-thirty at the Savoy,' he said, glancing at his watch. 'I suppose we should be on our way; we mustn't be late or we won't have time for dinner before the show.'

Relieved, Gina got up and walked across the room to get her coat, deeply aware of the fact that Nick was watching the instinctive sway of her supple body in the elegant little black crêpe dress she was wearing. It was the sort of dress you could wear on any occasion and it made a perfect foil for her vivid russet hair and slanting green eyes.

Nick caught up with her as she reached up for her coat, and held it out for her; she hurriedly slid her arms into it, very conscious of him standing so close behind her, the scent of his aftershave musky. He bent forward before she could move away, pushing aside her hair, his mouth brushing her nape and whispered, 'You look very sexy in that dress, Gina.'

She tried to keep cool, but knew that her tense awareness of him hadn't passed him by. Nick knew what he could do to her when he came so close, used that deep, smoky, whispering voice, let his lips touch her skin. All her senses were working overtime, reacting to him.

'If we weren't in such a hurry I'd have to do something about that,' Nick said softly. 'But it will have to wait.'

Gina felt him step away to get his own coat; relief made her tremble as she made for the door, opened it, stood waiting while Nick wound a white silk scarf around his throat, buttoned up his smooth cashmere coat, drew on elegant black leather gloves.

He had said she looked sexy. That went for him, too, she thought, lowering her lashes and swallowing. Nick always looked sexy, but especially in evening dress; the dark suit and white shirt gave him an air that made him irresistible.

His white Rolls-Royce was waiting outside Barbary Wharf, drawn up in front of the main gate. His chauffeur always drove him when he had an evening appointment so that Nick did not have the problem of finding somewhere to park. Gina climbed into the back of the limousine carefully, still very aware of Nick watching her slender, silk-clad legs as she sank into the seat.

'The Savoy, as fast as you can get there,' he told his chauffeur, and then he bent his long body to get in beside her and as he did Gina heard a strange, loud sound, like a firecracker going off. At the same time she saw an orange flash of light, heard somebody screaming, heard people running, a car engine revving noisily near by.

Gina was dazed, bewildered. What on earth was going on? Time seemed to have slowed down in an extraordinary way; as if every second ticked by endlessly, as if she was in a film which rolled frame by frame, dragged out to the end of time. She was staring at Nick's face, framed in the open door of the car. He looked so odd: blank, white. His mouth was open. She had the feeling he was shouting, or screaming, but she couldn't hear him making a sound. He was still bending forwards, his hands outstretched.

And then time speeded up again. Outside in the street a man carrying a gun jumped into the car which was running its engine noisily; the car drove away with a screech of tyres.

Nick crashed forwards into the back of the white Rolls-Royce, and fell on his face at her feet; while she stared down at him in horror and shock, a thin streak of red blood slid down his face from under his black hair.

CHAPTER SEVEN

GINA fell on her knees beside him, groaning his name. 'Nick...Nick...' He was dead, she knew he was dead. She touched his face and it was already cold; she couldn't hear him breathing, touched his lips and felt them wet. She stared at her fingers, retching. They were red with Nick's blood.

'Gawd almighty,' the chauffeur said behind her, standing at the door staring down at Nick's body. 'Is he dead?'

'I don't know...' Gina whispered hoarsely, but she believed he was. She had lost James to violent death. It had taught her to expect tragedy; fear paralysed her.

'Did you see the guy? He had a gun, he come out of nowhere, one minute he wasn't there, then he was...I saw it all. I couldn't make out what was happening, he had something in his hand but I couldn't see what...till he shot the boss...'

Gina looked round. His face was white under the peak of his uniform cap; his eyes dark, dilated with shock. He was clutching the door-handle and his hands were trembling; he was trembling from head to foot. She could hear his teeth chattering as he stared down at Nick.

'Must think, do something...' Gina muttered, pulling herself together. She slid her hand down Nick's throat, feeling for a pulse without much hope, and stiffened. Under her fingers she had picked up a thread of movement. She pressed down into his neck. Yes, there it was, a pulse, beating erratically. Nick was still alive.

Everything changed. Gina took a long, agonised breath. 'He's alive! I've picked up a pulse. Help me move his legs into the car.'

'I don't think you ought, miss...madam,' stammered the chauffeur. 'You're not supposed to move someone who's been badly hurt. I've read that. We ought to ring for an ambulance and wait 'ere. Keep 'im warm, like.' He looked around wildly, then with a sudden start burst out, 'The car phone...that's what we need.'

People had begun to cluster on the pavement, although Gina was scarcely aware of them.

'We haven't got time,' she said desperately. 'It would take an ambulance too long to get here; we can get him to the nearest hospital in a few minutes! Come on, just lift his legs in, we'll try not to move his head, that's...' Her voice broke, she swallowed, then hoarsely went on, 'That's where he was shot!'

The wound was visible; a confused mass of hair and blood on the back of his head. She averted her eyes from it, feeling sick.

'Mrs Tyrrell, he'll get jolted about something awful! We shouldn't, really we shouldn't,' the chauffeur persisted, but she gave him a terrible look, her green eyes glittering with the insistence of desperation.

'Do as you're told, will you? You're wasting time arguing!'

The chauffeur's face stiffened and reddened. Then someone from the crowd came forward silently to help. Gina recognised one of the electricians from the printing works. Together he and the chauffeur gently lifted Nick's long legs up into the back of the car, carefully curled them round so that he lay in a foetal position on the floor.

Gina sat down beside his head, to support him if he shifted, but afraid to raise his head even enough to push a cushion underneath it, in case that was the wrong thing to do. She pushed one of the leather car seats in behind his back in an effort to hold him in that position, make sure he didn't roll with the movement of the car.

'Now, drive steadily, but get us there as fast as you safely can,' she said huskily to the chauffeur.

The man still hadn't given up. He gave her an obstinate, sullen look. 'Well, if you're taking responsibility, Mrs Tyrrell...I don't think we should move him but if you're giving me an order I'll drive you there!'

Gina gave the man a level stare. 'I take full responsibility. Will you get behind that wheel and stop arguing?' Then she managed a faint smile for the electrician beside him. 'Thanks.'

He nodded. 'We'll ring ahead and tell the casualty department you're coming,' he promised, before he closed the door.

It was a nightmare drive for Gina. She felt every tiny bump they hit, every swerve of the car around a corner. She was half lying beside Nick, her arm over him, cradling him, watching him intently for any sign of a change in his condition, but he was still unconscious when the Rolls pulled up at the hospital casualty department a short time later.

They had been alerted, they were waiting, two men in white coats and a couple of nurses, a porter with a stretcher. They took over with the speed of people accustomed to doing this every day of their lives. The doctor grunted questions as he swiftly examined Nick before they switched him to the stretcher. But he hardly waited for her answers before firing new questions at her.

'A shooting?'

'Yes, that's——'

'In the head?'

'Yes, as far as I can——'

'No other wounds?'

'I don't think——'

'How long ago did it happen?'

Blankly, she looked at her watch, in stupid confusion. 'I don't know.' So much had happened that time had unrolled with lightning speed, she couldn't believe it when she saw the hands of her watch. It was just on half-past six. They had walked out of their office at a quarter past; just fifteen minutes ago. At the Savoy Nick's mother and sister would be waiting, expecting them at any minute.

Remembering them made her burst out, 'Oh, his mother...I must let his mother know what's happened...'

At the same time the chauffeur was gruffly saying, 'It happened just on twenty past six. I told her we shouldn't move him, but she insisted. I told her...'

The doctor glanced at Gina.

'I was afraid the ambulance would take too long,' she said, her eyes afraid. 'Have I harmed his chances...?'

'In this case, no, don't worry,' the doctor said. 'But it isn't ever a good idea to move a wounded person until a doctor has seen him.'

The chauffeur gave her the look of a man who had been justified, but Gina was only intent on Nick, and so was the doctor.

'Has he been unconscious ever since it happened?'

'Yes, is that a bad sign? It is, isn't it?' Gina was so scared that her voice was shaking.

The doctor gave her a sharp, searching look. 'What about you?'

'Me?' she said blankly, then realised what he was getting at. 'No, I wasn't shot, there's nothing wrong with me.'

'Hmm...you'd better stay around, anyway, until I have time to look at you,' he said, and then the whole party moved off at a run, taking Nick with them, and Gina ran after them.

As she hurried across the tiled floor of the hospital casualty department a uniformed policeman ran after her and caught her by the arm.

'Hang on a minute, miss, I need a few details from you.'

She stared after the stretcher. Nick was covered by a blanket now, but she could see his dark hair blowing about as they wheeled him into a curtained cubicle.

'I want to go with him!'

'They won't let you. They know what they're doing, don't worry. The doctors here get all sorts of accidents in every day, he's in very good hands, Miss... what is your name, miss?'

'Mrs,' she said blankly. 'Mrs Tyrrell.'

The policeman wrote busily. 'His wife?'

'No, we aren't married.'

'I see,' he said in what was meant to be a soothing voice. 'Well, first things first... what's his name?'

'Caspian,' said Gina flatly. 'Nick Caspian.'

His pen poised over his notebook, the policeman stared. 'The newspaper owner?'

She nodded. She had begun to feel very odd. The floor was behaving very strangely; going up and down, as if it were breathing, or as if she stood on the deck of a ship on a stormy sea. Gina's head swam. She swayed, staring down at the floor, her skin creeping, afraid that she was going to throw up at any minute.

'Weird,' she said, and fell forward against the policeman's blue uniformed chest.

When she opened her eyes she was lying on a bed. She stared up at a cracked and yellowing ceiling. Where on earth was she? Her gaze shifted sideways and saw dull green curtains all around her, swaying and dipping. Her bewilderment deepened. For a few more seconds she couldn't remember what she was doing there, what had happened: her mind was a total blank. Then somebody moved, cleared his throat.

'How do you feel now, Mrs Tyrrell?' said a calm, unhurried voice, and Gina recognised it, and with the recognition her memory came back in one blinding rush.

'Nick...somebody shot Nick...' she whispered, then, childishly, 'Did I faint?'

'Yes, but there's nothing to worry about! One of the nurses took a look at you and said you were OK, it was just shock. They're going to keep you in overnight, in case, but they haven't got a bed ready yet, so they put you in here and said I could stay with you. They're rushed off their feet out there.'

'What's happening to Nick?' She sat up and tried to swing her legs down, but the policeman jumped to restrain her, his face concerned.

'They're looking after him; nothing you can do, you know...do you feel OK? Can I get you anything?'

She was feeling very shaky so she lay down again. 'A cup of tea?' It was all she could think of, but the policeman relaxed, smiling. She had said the right thing, the thing he expected.

'That's what they always want! Coming up. Sugar? Milk?'

'Please.'

As he turned to go out through the curtains she said urgently, 'Can you ask about Nick? Please, I must know how he is...'

'I was going to ask anyway. Now, you stay where you are! You aren't to move.' The curtain fell back behind him and she stared at the green cloth billowing like smoke. She felt as if she was trapped in a nightmare; there was something so shabbily ordinary about this place and yet it was desolate, the air was thick with fear and pain.

The policeman came back carrying two paper cups of tea. Gina sat up, and he handed her one.

She held it between her cold, trembling hands, glad of the warmth as he told her what he had found out.

'They've already whisked him up to Theatre. They're always cagey, but a nurse I know quite well said it wasn't really serious, he would be OK.'

Gina stared; she didn't really believe him but at least Nick was still alive.

'Drink up your tea, Mrs Tyrrell, then I'm afraid I must ask you a few questions about the incident.'

Gina sipped her tea gratefully, feeling a little better with its warmth inside her, then she told him everything she knew, which wasn't much. She hadn't really seen the gunman. She explained that she had been inside the car; all she had seen was Nick, at the moment that he was hit. Wearily she described the sounds she had heard, the car that had been waiting for the gunman and picked him up before driving away very fast.

'The chauffeur probably saw more than I did. Is he still here?'

'Yes, one of my colleagues is talking to him.' He looked at her searchingly. 'Mrs Tyrrell, are you sure you didn't see the man with the gun?'

'Just a shape, a dark shape...he stood out of the light from the street-lamps...'

'How tall would you say he was?' He took her through a minute catechism for several minutes and Gina answered as best she could, but all her attention had been riveted on Nick, and she hardly remembered anything else.

'One last question, Mrs Tyrrell, do you know anyone who might want to kill Mr Caspian? Anyone with a grievance against him, or who had threatened him?'

'Yes, I knew at once, when it happened. I'd been afraid of something like this,' Gina said, and told him about Tom Birny's East End Mafia families articles, and the threats that had been made against him, and Nick.

'Where could I get in touch with this Mr Birny tonight?' the policeman asked.

Gina shook her head dumbly for a second, then realised that she had her address book in her bag. She fumbled for it, found Tom's address and telephone number and gave them to the policeman.

'I begged him to get protection, and he laughed! He wouldn't take it seriously, neither of them would. Tom was just as bad, he just shrugged the threats off...' Then she stopped dead, her eyes widening. 'Tom! Oh, you must find him, before they do! If they tried to kill Nick they'll try to kill Tom!'

The policeman was already on his way. 'I'll find him, don't worry,' he said. 'You just rest, Mrs Tyrrell. They'll come and tell you as soon as there's any news.'

When he had gone Gina slid down from the bed, realising she was barefoot. They had removed her shoes and she couldn't find them under the bed. While she was searching on hands and knees someone came through the curtains and said, 'And what do you think you're doing?'

Gina got up. 'Looking for my shoes,' she said, recognising the doctor who had admitted Nick. 'Is he still in Theatre? What are they doing to him? Do you think he's going to be all right?'

'He's on the operating table now; they're tidying up his head...'

Gina winced and he smiled at her.

'Did that sound alarming? It isn't. He's a very lucky man, in fact. The bullet creased along his scalp but didn't penetrate the brain, there is a lot of blood but he won't need major surgery, just a tidying operation, cleaning out the surface wound and stitching where necessary.'

Gina couldn't believe it, her green eyes dazed. 'But... he was unconscious so long...'

'Ah, that was because he hit his head when he fell, I think. He has a very large contusion on his temples, nothing at all to do with the gunshot wound. He may have concussion, but the X-rays showed no brain damage at all. As I said, a very lucky man.' He took her elbow in a firm hand. 'Now, hop back on here and let me take a look at you. Where did you think you were going, by the way? I told you, I'd like you to stay here overnight, in case of shock—the after-effects of something like this can be quite nasty, you know.'

'I have to ring his mother. She was meeting us at the Savoy for dinner, and she's probably still waiting, I must let her know what's happened.'

'I'll get you a phone,' the doctor said, striding off. He came back a couple of minutes later with a portable telephone and plugged it into a socket on the wall. 'Here you are, make your call. I'll come back in five minutes to take a look at you.'

'Oh, thank you!'

Gina first rang Directory Enquiries to get the number for the Savoy hotel and then rang them, asking if they could page Mrs Caspian who would most probably be waiting in the bar of the River Room.

There was a wait of several minutes before she heard Mrs Caspian's voice. 'Nick?' she anxiously enquired and Gina bit her lip.

'No, Mrs Caspian, it's me, Gina. I'm afraid there has been an accident...'

She hard the intake of breath, then Mrs Caspian whispered, 'Nick's hurt? Is it serious? Is——?'

'He's going to be OK,' Gina quickly assured, and Mrs Caspian let out a long sigh.

'Was he driving that sports car? I've told him a hundred times that he drives too fast...'

Gina didn't know how to tell her the truth, the shock might do something drastic to the older woman's heart, which Gina knew was not strong.

'He's having minor surgery at the moment, but they tell me it should be over any minute now. You won't be able to see him for a while, so there is no point in coming here tonight; you could see him tomorrow. Why not have something to eat and then go on to the theatre?'

'No, I won't bother, I couldn't enjoy myself. I'll just go home and watch television for an hour, then get an early night.'

Gina thought quickly. 'Is Alessa there with you? Could I have a word with her?'

'Alessa? Yes, she's here.' Mrs Caspian sounded startled. 'I'll put on her.'

Alessa said drily, 'I gather my dear brother crashed his car? How badly? Were you hurt?'

'No, I'm fine, but, listen, Alessa, I didn't know how to tell your mother, and I'm afraid she may see the news on television and find out, and it would be a bad shock for her. You see, the truth is, Nick didn't crash his car; he's been shot.'

'What?' Alessa's voice was shocked.

'Careful, don't say anything that might upset your mother,' Gina urged. 'You'll have to break it to her gently. I wouldn't want her to collapse.'

Slowly Alessa asked, 'What exactly happened?'

'The *Sentinel* crime reporter has been running a series of articles exposing East End gangland families and their connections—the reporter was threatened, Nick was threatened, but neither of them took the threats seriously.'

'Typical!' Alessa grimly said and Gina agreed.

'Absolutely. Nick refused to get protection——'

'His pride wouldn't let him take it seriously.'

'His ego, you mean,' Gina said. 'That whole male thing...their ideas about machismo and being strong...it makes them do such stupid things. If Nick had only taken some down-to-earth precautions! But no! He would have seen that as admitting he was afraid, so he wouldn't even discuss it!' She gave a short, angry sigh. 'And then tonight as we were leaving to meet you someone shot him. Whoever it was, wasn't a very good shot; they fired any number of times and only hit Nick once, and, even then, they tell me he was lucky; the bullet only creased his scalp, causing a lot of blood but no damage to the brain.'

'Thank God for that,' breathed Alessa.

'Yes,' Gina said, tears in her eyes. 'They're operating now to clean the wound and stitch it up, but he's in no danger, they assure me.'

'When you think what could have happened...' Alessa muttered.

Gina couldn't bear to think about it. 'He gave me the biggest scare of my life tonight. I could kill him when I remember what I went through! I didn't know if he was alive or dead and I was helpless, there was nothing I could do to save him if he was dying...I'm so angry with him, Alessa!'

'Poor Gina, you have had a bad time!' Alessa said, warmly sympathetic. 'Where are you ringing from? Are you back home now?'

'No, I'm still at the hospital; they're keeping me in overnight. They say I might be in shock.'

'I suspect they're right,' said Alessa in her light, wry tones, a smile in her voice too. 'Well, you get some sleep and we'll be in to see you tomorrow. I'll take my mother back to Nick's apartment and tell her all about it there, so don't worry about that.'

Gina rang off and lay down again, feeling abruptly very tired indeed. The doctor returned and looked down at her.

'How do you feel?'

'Tired.' She couldn't stop a terrific yawn, flapping a hand over her mouth. 'Sorry.'

'Bed for you,' said the doctor and she didn't argue with him. By the time she had been undressed and was in bed in a large ward full of other women she was already half asleep, but the night nurse gave her a sleeping pill anyway, and when Gina woke up again it was to find the long room full of grey, wintry daylight.

She had a cup of tea and some cornflakes, refused a cooked breakfast, saw the doctor a short time later and was discharged.

'Can I see Nick before I go?' she asked, and the doctor shrugged.

'Go up and ask his ward sister. I don't dare give you permission if she isn't willing to let you see him outside visiting hours. It ruins the day for them, you know, if their routines are upset.'

Gina dressed and found her way through the interminable corridors to the men's surgical ward where a short, brisk young woman in immaculate uniform gave her reluctant permission to see Nick. 'Just for five minutes, though! You can come back at visiting time.'

He was in a private one-bed room off the main ward and was already sitting up, a white bandage around his head, wearing dark blue and white striped cotton pyjamas which were obviously hospital issue! They had a distinct resemblance to prison garb.

When she opened the door, his grey eyes flashed to her urgently. 'Gina! Are you OK? I kept asking but nobody would tell me.'

'I'm fine,' she reassured him, walking across the room while he watched her.

'You're still wearing the same dress!'

'The hospital made me stay overnight, I'm just going home now.' Gina looked at him hard. 'How do you feel this morning?'

'I've got a headache,' he joked, then made a peremptory gesture. 'Don't stand there as if you're leaving any second. You can surely stay for five minutes! Bring that chair over here and sit down.'

She gave him a rueful look. 'I can see you're yourself again! Giving orders left, right and centre.' But she obeyed, and as she sat down, his hand reached out to capture hers.

Gina let his strong fingers envelop hers; looked down at them twined together, his still faintly tanned from his constant visits to sunnier climes, hers pale and slender. She could feel Nick's skin warm against her own, saw the blue vein in his wrist where his blood beat; it was unbearably moving. He was alive, and could so easily have been killed last night.

'You should never have taken such risks!' she said, her anger suddenly rising up through her like mercury in a thermometer. 'You could have been killed! From now on you must have a bodyguard, everywhere you go! These men may try again. Maybe you should leave London? Go abroad for a few months?'

'Don't get so agitated!' he calmed, his thumb stroking the back of her hand. 'I've already made arrangements for some protection, when I leave here. But I'm not being driven out of London. I'm not going to let these people win. In any case, the police have already picked up several suspects. They came to see me half an hour ago, to take a statement. They got the number of the get-away car from someone who saw the whole thing; it was a stolen car but by sheer luck when they abandoned it and drove off in another car they were seen by a police car who chased them half through the East End until they crashed into a lamp-post. The guy who made such a hash of trying to kill me was killed himself; the driver got off with a few scratches and is in custody. They turned out to be from one of the East End families Tom Birny has been writing about, and the police rounded up a number of other members of the gang.'

Gina frowned. 'Tom...I'd forgotten Tom...they didn't try to kill him, too, did they?'

'Tom left London yesterday afternoon,' Nick drily said. 'For a couple of weeks' holiday at my family villa on Martinique.'

Gina sighed. 'Thank heavens for that!'

Nick smiled at her. 'And thanks for letting my mother know so promptly, it was thoughtful of you. I talked to her on the phone this morning, to set her mind at rest, so that she could see I hadn't been badly injured. She's coming in to see me this afternoon, but then I'm sending her back to San Francisco in the company jet. I don't want her at risk.' He gave Gina a level, serious look. 'Gina, I think you should go away for a while, too, until this thing is settled. You haven't had a holiday for ages, you need some sunshine. Get someone to go with you... Roz, maybe?'

'I've got too much to do,' she impatiently argued. 'And so has Roz! I can't ask her to give up some of her holiday quota, for my sake!'

Nick leaned towards her angrily; face insistent, his blue-striped pyjamas gaping open at the throat, showing her his pale tanned skin. Gina looked, then looked away, breathless suddenly.

'I must know you're safe, Gina! Promise you'll go,' Nick said. 'Look, if my mother is back in San Francisco my sister Alessa could go with you—will you go, if she does?'

'I can't ask your sister to come on holiday with me at a moment's notice! We hardly know each other.'

'She likes you, she wants to get to know you better,' said Nick quickly. 'I'll talk to her—if she says yes, will you go?'

How could she refuse?

CHAPTER EIGHT

Two weeks later Gina arrived back in London on a flight from Cairo, feeling terrible. It had been a long flight, they had met turbulence halfway, been flung around the sky like a toy in the hands of a rough child, and Gina, in common with many other passengers, had thrown up. She still felt weak-legged, especially when she saw Nick waiting for her. She hadn't expected that.

As he strode to meet her Gina looked at him fixedly, anxiously. While she was away she had kept waking up from nightmares, reliving those moments when he was shot and fell at her feet. He had been white and drawn last time she saw him—but now, to her intense relief, he seemed to be himself again, a tough, exciting male animal in that beautifully tailored suit, at whom people stared in fascination as he walked past them.

'Hello,' she said, stupidly breathless when he reached her.

'Hello,' he said in a deep, warm voice, smiling, and for a few seconds they just looked at each other. Gina felt a surge of happiness, of homecoming, as though just to have him there had made her world complete.

Nick took over the loaded luggage trolley she was pushing. 'What on earth have you got in all those cases? Don't tell me you've brought back souvenirs—not those awful fake Egyptian antiquities?'

'Yes,' she said, laughing defiantly. 'The Egyptian souvenir sellers loved me; I was the perfect tourist, I couldn't resist fake jade necklaces and cheap replicas of Tutankhamun's tomb jewellery.'

He looked amused, his grey eyes sliding over her in a leisurely, sensual enjoyment which made her blush.

'Your trip seems to have done you good. That's a great tan you've got, it suits you.'

Flushed, she said, 'Thanks, but you should have seen me last week! I looked like a lobster. I only started getting any sort of tan a couple of days ago.'

Gina's red hair and pale skin did not take the sun easily. She had found Egypt's heat enervating, and had learnt to stay out of the sun as much as possible.

She had also learnt to carry a fly whisk and flick it about, but that hadn't helped keep off the little boys begging her to buy cheap jewellery. She had found it hard to resist their huge dark eyes and pleading wails, to Alessa's disgusted amusement.

From one street salesman she had acquired her best buy of the trip—a long white caftan with a hood; she found it kept her cooler than Western clothes did, and it hid the vivid russet hair which made her such a target with the Egyptian men, who went into raptures over her red hair.

'Had a good flight?' asked Nick as they walked out of the building into a cold February sunlight which made Gina shiver, realising fully then that she was back in winter after the brazen heat of Egypt.

'We ran into a storm. It was hair-raising. I thought my last hour had come, for a while, but we flew on out of it.'

'I hate flying through bad weather.' He gave her a sideways grin. 'Were you sick? I would have been.'

'Yes, I was,' she admitted, and their eyes met in shared laughter. There it was again—that new intimacy between them. She didn't know how or when it had grown but maybe it was because of the shared trauma of that moment when he was shot?

'Nothing else has happened while I was away?' she asked anxiously, watching him. 'No more threats?'

He shook his head. 'The police think they've got the guy behind the hit on me, and they don't expect the other gang members to risk a second try. Don't worry, I'm safe, I've had security shadowing me everywhere I went for the last two weeks and they were certain I wasn't being watched or followed.'

'But where are they now?' Gina asked, looking around as they reached his Rolls.

'I told them to tag behind us in another car. Now, don't worry! There's no danger any more.'

'That's what you said last time!' she muttered. He seemed to have recovered completely; outwardly there was nothing to tell you what had happened but she knew she would never forget that terrible day, nor the moments when she had thought Nick was dead.

His colour was good now, though, and his black hair was carefully brushed over the place where he had been shot and later operated on, leaving, Mrs Caspian had told Alessa on the phone, a bald patch.

Alessa had said to Gina, 'Poor old Nick, he was horrified when he found it, but the doctors say it will grow again. Mama said he could always become a monk, as he has a tonsure now, but he didn't think that was funny.'

His sister's irreverent laughter had also helped to change the way Gina felt towards him. It was hard to hate someone you had giggled over.

'It's very thoughtful of you to meet me,' she said politely, as his chauffeur stowed her luggage into the back of Nick's limousine. 'Did your mother tell you which plane I was taking?'

'Yes. Why didn't *you*?'

'It never occurred to me,' she lied, and Nick gave her a sardonic look as he helped her into the car and slid in beside her.

Being shut up with him in that circumscribed space gave her claustrophobia. It was hard to breathe; her heart was beating worryingly fast. Nick shifted closer, crossing one leg over the other, turning towards her, one arm along the back of the seat in an intimate, lounging gesture which made her nerves worse.

'Alessa talked to Mama on the phone last night, from Cairo, and said she was going on to Martinique, to paint, as Tom Birny was due to move out of the villa this weekend and it would be free for her. She suggested that Mama might care to join her there, but Mama has had a touch of flu, and is staying in bed to recover.'

'Yes, Alessa told me,' Gina huskily said. 'I hope your mother is being well looked after by the woman you found to replace Mrs Grant?'

'I hope so, Mama seems to like Mrs Ferris. I haven't met her myself yet, but she had excellent references and Mama says she's very competent—she's an ex-nurse— but I suspect she won't stay long. She's only thirty, much too young for the job. She's from New York, she's getting divorced and wanted to move to California to get away from her ex-husband, but I think she'll get bored in a few months and leave. In the meantime, it's working out quite well. The main thing is, my mother likes her.'

Gina watched Nick's serious face, touched by the amount of care he always gave to anything concerned with his mother. Becoming aware of her stare, his gaze shot to her face, his grey eyes narrowing.

'How did you and Alessa get on?'

'Like a house on fire!'

'Really?' He seemed surprised. Maybe he had expected her to take a dislike to Alessa, just because she was his sister? Well, he couldn't be more wrong. They had become good friends during their two weeks in Egypt, cruising along the Nile in a leisurely fashion, on an elegant old paddle-steamer which had been luxuriously modernised.

Each day after a light breakfast at first light they had left the boat to visit archaeological sites, returning aboard for lunch. Days had been busy and tiring, and in the evenings after dinner everyone went along to the salon, which was furnished as it would have been at the turn of the century, with a grand piano, brocade curtains, dark red Axminster carpets, Arab prayer rugs hanging on the walls, glass globe Victorian table-lamps, comfortable armchairs with velvet cushions in them, and scattered green baize card tables.

'Were there many other people on board?' asked Nick.

'There were a couple of dozen of us all told, I think.'

'Mostly couples?'

Gina didn't miss the note in his voice; she gave him a secretive look through lowered lashes.

'Mostly,' she agreed blandly.

'And much older than you and Alessa, too, I imagine? The sort of people who take these trips are usually middle-aged or older.'

She nodded. 'Most of them were older.' They had twice had a musical evening, a singer accompanied by a pianist—otherwise the guests tended either to go to bed early or to play cards in concentrated silence at the green baize tables, unaware of their surroundings.

Nick relaxed, smiling, the arm resting along the back of the seat curling around her as he bent closer.

'Oh, well, it must have been restful,' he began but Gina hadn't finished speaking.

'Luckily, there were one or two younger men!'

'Men?' Nick repeated, frowning.

'There was our tutor, Dr Heath ... he was about the same age as Alessa, and very attractive.'

'Oh, was he?' Nick scowled.

'And the tour courier, Julian—he was more my age and he has been taking these parties down the Nile for a couple of years. He said he couldn't believe his luck when he saw me and Alessa walking on board.'

Nick gave her an acid smile. 'I hope you aren't going to tell me you had a holiday romance!'

Gina laughed. 'You told me to get away from everything and enjoy myself! Well, Alessa and I had a great time.'

What she didn't tell him was that Dr Heath was married with several small children and had had no interest in either her or Alessa except as members of his tour party, nor that Julian had been a small, skinny, untidy young man who was kept busy trying to placate people with complaints about the food, the service, the heat, the flies, or a hundred other things.

Most evenings, Gina and Alessa grew bored with the card-players and the stuffy air in the salon, and went out to walk around the deck under a starry Egyptian sky, watching the moon climb the heavens, washing the desert with liquid silver, and talking about life, men, their families, men, their careers, and men.

Gina knew she would never forget the landscapes of the Nile they floated past while they talked in ever-decreasing circles. The images shimmered in her mind's eye—the bullrushes and reeds, the muddy banks, the palm trees, an ox plodding in a circle, muddy water pumping up and out into the dust, baked-mud villages, often just one dusty street, with chickens pecking in the roots of trees and children playing outside the flat-roofed, white-washed houses with their ovens and dovecots on the roof, fields of alfalfa grass, suntanned men in well-washed unbleached robes, riding donkeys laden with alfalfa. These scenes were strangely familiar to her at first sight: and then she remembered where she had seen them before—faded brown illustrations in old bibles.

Each day, there was a breathtaking moment when the fiery orange sun sank suddenly into a dark blueness and night came with a rush. At dawn, the sun rose again as suddenly, filling the skies with fire.

At night they heard strange, disturbing sounds: the howl of jackals in the desert, the leather rattle of wings as dusk fell and bats streamed out of their haunted places

among the tombs, the flap of a heron coming to fish
among the reeds, the long, unearthly wail of the muezzin,
calling the faithful to prayer from one of the hundreds
of mosques they passed.

Egypt was a strange mixture of the very ancient and
the ultra-modern: skyscrapers, fast trains and traffic jams
in Cairo on the one hand and on the other the peasant
life in the Nile delta, which did not appear to have
changed since the days of the Pharoahs.

'Well, you've obviously come back very pleased with
yourself!' said Nick, watching her.

'I'm very glad I went, if that's what you mean,' Gina
said, brought back to the present. 'I really got to know
Alessa; we talked for hours.'

'About Egypt?'

She gave him a demure little smile. 'That too.'

'Hmm,' said Nick thoughtfully. 'Why the cat-that-
swallowed-the-cream look? What has Alessa been telling
you?'

'Let's just say she gave me a sisterly view of you,'
Gina teased him as the limousine pulled up outside their
apartment block. The porter saw them arrive and hurried
out to collect her suitcases from the chauffeur.

'I'll bring them up at once, Mrs Tyrrell!'

'Thank you.' Gina smiled at him and he beamed back.

'I can see you got lots of sun in Egypt. Wish I'd gone
with you. We've had terrible weather here—rained nearly
every day, and as cold as charity most of the time.'

'It was too hot for me,' said Gina, and out of the
corner of her eye saw Nick scowling and fidgeting, impatient with the delay. He was not a man who chatted
with porters and taxi drivers. He was always preoccupied with more important things; in a hurry to get
somewhere, do something. Nick was a driven man. He
had surely exceeded any dreams he or his father might
have had for the Caspian empire. And yet...and yet

Nick was never satisfied, never able to rest. He was as taut as a drawn bow.

On their way up to the top floor in the lift Nick said offhandedly, 'A lot has happened while you were in Egypt. We must have dinner tonight so that I can tell you all about it.'

She didn't refuse. Giving him a wry look, she said, 'What time?'

'I'll call for you at seven. Until then, don't start unpacking and putting stuff away—you ought to rest. That must have been a tiring flight.'

'The first thing I'm going to do is have a long, hot bath! Then I'll lie down on my bed for a couple of hours.'

She took Nick's advice and left her unpacking—it could be done tomorrow. She ran a bath, poured in sweet-scented bath salts, stripped off and climbed into the water with a groan of pleasure. Her muscles had been tensed throughout the flight; she felt them relax in the warmth of the bath and lay back, eyes closed, her mind drifting away. She was very glad she had gone to Egypt. Not only had she enjoyed those two weeks and felt that she and Alessa were real friends now, but also although Nick had not been there she had found out a great deal about him that she would not otherwise ever have guessed. Alessa had private memories of her brother as a child, as a boy, as a young man—Gina had been able to see him from a dozen different angles.

She reluctantly climbed out of her bath at last, dried herself, and put on a pale green striped towelling robe. She made herself some China tea and carried it into the bedroom to drink; then curled up on top of her bed, pulled a light rug over herself and was soon asleep.

The sound of the phone woke her; starting up, she automatically reached out and hit her bedside lamp, which rocked wildly but didn't fall. The room was dark; she put on the light, glancing at the clock as she then picked up the phone; it was nearly six. She must have slept for an hour and a half.

'Hello?' she said and Roz's voice answered.

'Gina! You *are* back. Sophie said she thought you were due back today—why didn't you let me know? We'd have met you.'

'I thought you'd be working; I didn't want to bother you. How are the wedding plans coming along?'

'Well, the guest list keeps growing as Daniel's family come up with more and more relatives who must be invited, but otherwise everything's fine. So, how was your holiday? What did you think of Egypt? Wasn't I right about the heat and the flies and the bazaar sellers?'

'Absolutely right, but I loved the place. It was like walking into a dream.'

'I'm glad you enjoyed it. Look, the reason I'm calling is . . . Piet rang the office this afternoon——'

'Piet?' Gina gave a little gasp of surprised excitement. 'Hazel's had the baby?'

Roz laughed. 'You're quick!'

'What was it? How's Hazel?'

'A boy, and Hazel's fine,' said Roz, amused. 'Piet was like a dog with two tails; you'd never think anyone had ever had a baby before. He said he'd tried to ring you and got no reply so he rang the office to leave a message with Sophie and I happened to be there so I had a chat with him. He says Hazel was only in labour around six hours, and had no trouble at all. The baby was only just five pounds; it was early.'

'I thought it was! Maybe moving to Holland, all that upheaval, started labour early? It must have been quite a wrench for her, leaving England for good.'

'Maybe,' Roz agreed.

'Have they thought of a name yet?'

'Piet wants to call him Nicholas—how do you think Nick will react to that?'

'Nick and he have been friends for years!' Gina rather defensively pointed out, not really surprised.

'Until Piet announced he was leaving Caspian International and setting up on his own! Don't tell me Nick didn't see that as treachery, because I know the man. He has a very retentive memory.'

'Oh, he was cross for a while, but I'm sure he's over it now.'

'Hmm, I wonder?' Roz said cynically. 'Well, I think Piet will ask him to stand as godfather to the baby, too. I'll be interested to see if he accepts. Shall we have a bet on it? Five pounds says he refuses.'

'I don't gamble,' Gina said with dignity, and Roz hooted derisively.

'You mean you aren't prepared to risk it! Come on, put your money where your mouth is! If you really believe Nick isn't a grudge-bearer, that is!'

'OK, I will!' said Gina, more furious because Roz was right, she wasn't sure how Nick would react when he heard about the baby, than because she thought Roz was being unfair to Nick.

After she had rung off she had to hurry to get ready for dinner with Nick. She still felt the chill of English weather after her weeks in Egypt, so she put on a dress she had bought in Paris at one of the new, young designer houses—a warm mustard-coloured wool dress with long sleeves, small gold buttons to the waist and a sleekly fitting straight skirt.

When Nick arrived, promptly at seven, Gina opened the door to him with the news about Hazel's baby. She didn't tell him that Roz had said Piet wanted to name the baby after him, or that Piet might ask him to stand godfather to the baby—and certainly not that she and Roz had a bet on whether he would accept.

'I know, Piet rang me too,' he said, his grey eyes restlessly moving over her slender figure in the smoothly fitting wool dress. 'They're calling the baby Nicholas and they've asked me to be godfather—Piet said Hazel wants you to be godmother too, so we can go over together for the ceremony.'

Gina gave him a brilliant smile, her eyes very bright, and Nick did a double-take, then his eyes narrowed on her with faint suspicion.

'Why the grin?'

'I'm just so thrilled about Hazel's baby,' she evaded, since she couldn't tell him that he had just helped her win five pounds. 'Where are we going tonight?'

'A little French restaurant I know,' he said, mischief in his face, and Gina wasn't surprised when she found herself walking into Pierre's ten minutes later. The restaurant was half-empty; they were given Nick's usual table in a discreet corner, masked from the rest of the room by a low dividing wall.

'I'm going to have tonight's special, the *boeuf en croute*,' Nick decided after studying the menu. 'What about you?'

She grimaced in horror. 'Much too high in calories for me! The beef is fine, but all that pastry! No, I'll just have the poached salmon, and I'll start with this melon cascade—they do that so well.'

'Yes, I'll start with that, too,' Nick nodded. He picked up the wine list and began studying that. 'We'll have some white wine with the melon and then I'll have some red with my beef, but you can stay with the white wine with your fish, or join me with the red.'

'I doubt if I'll drink more than one glass of wine, but I'd like some sparkling mineral water.' Gina fiddled with one of the small gold disc earrings matching her dress buttons, which had come loose, and Nick watched her intently, as if every little movement she made fascinated him.

The head waiter came over, bowed obsequiously to Nick, took their order and vanished again. Another waiter brought them the aperitifs Nick had ordered when they first arrived, and while Gina was sipping her kir, white wine flavoured with blackcurrant, Nick glanced over her shoulder and smiled, waving at someone.

Gina looked round and saw Colette Tse coming across the room. She was wearing Chinese dress tonight: a beautiful turquoise-blue silk tunic top and under that matching loose silk trousers. Her dark hair hung free down her shoulders, shining black, and long, tasselled diamond earrings swung against her softly flushed olive skin as she moved in a graceful, sinuous gliding walk.

'Colette,' Nick murmured softly, a little smile playing around his mouth. 'Looking stunning tonight, isn't she?'

Gina turned back to eye him derisively. She knew what he was up to now; deliberately trying to make her jealous. It wasn't going to work any more and her mocking stare told him so before she asked, 'How's her research for the book about your family coming along?'

Nick's mouth twisted; he leaned back in his chair, face bland. 'Ah. You know about the book? Alessa, I suppose?'

'Alessa told me all sorts of things,' said Gina, and Nick's grey eyes sharpened.

'Oh, did she? I must thank my sister for that, when I see her! I told her to be discreet, watch what she said to you.'

'I know, she told me, but, as she said, you can give her orders but it doesn't follow that she'll obey them. You said you wanted me to make friends with your sister. I did. We got to know each other very well, and——'

She broke off as the waiter brought their first course: a melon shell, the fruit scooped out and then put back with a mixture of grapes, strawberries, kiwi fruit, slices of apple and orange and fresh pineapple, marinated in kirsch and fruit juice and spilling out in a cascade on to the plate, decorated with sprigs of mint.

'It looks too pretty to eat!' Gina told the waiter, who smiled.

'It tastes even better than it looks! *Bon appetit!*'

Gina took a spoonful and sighed. 'Oh, yes... it's delicious, isn't it?'

'Mmm,' said Nick. 'What were you about to say when he brought this?'

Gina gazed at him limpidly. 'Well, that Alessa couldn't explain why you didn't want me to know that Colette was writing a book about the Caspian family, and wanted to interview your mother and sisters, which was why Alessa and your mother came to London.' Let him wriggle out of that! she thought, giving him a dulcet smile.

'Colette doesn't want it to be public knowledge,' he surprised her by claiming.

He was as slippery as an eel! thought Gina. She might have guessed he would use Colette as an excuse.

Coolly, Nick went on, 'She wants to get the book finished and ready for publication before word gets out. She's afraid of being scooped, of other writers jumping on the bandwagon as soon as they hear what she's doing. Some of these hack biographers can write a book in a matter of weeks—they could get a book out before she can. She says she isn't naturally a fast writer; but she swears she's going to make a thorough job of the research before she so much as writes a word, and she's satisfied me that she will do the book well.'

'I'm sure she will, she's very capable,' Gina said fairly. She knew that Colette had a very good reputation on the paper, both as a features editor and as a writer herself. 'Although this is the first book she's ever done, to my knowledge.'

'Yes, she told me that, but she has specialised in writing character sketches up until now, and I saw her cuttings book; she has a good style and she isn't just a hack. When she approached me to ask for permission to write an official book on the family I hesitated at first and took time to think about it, and I only agreed to co-operate on certain conditions—firstly that I saw the manuscript before it even went to a publisher, second that I could insist on changes to any part of it I didn't like...'

Gina gazed at him with amusement. 'I can see you don't intend to take any chances!'

His eyes were hard and cool. 'Why should I allow her to write what she likes about me? I'm hoping that the very fact that this book has been published will deter other people from writing one.'

'Fat chance! It's more likely that it will excite the hack biographers into digging into your background to find out some scandal Colette hasn't dared use!'

'There isn't any,' said Nick coldly.

'Not even a few mistresses scattered around Europe?' she teased and his eyes glinted behind his dark lashes.

'Would it bother you if there were?'

'Why should I mind?' Gina asked innocently, opening her eyes wider.

Nick scowled, and went on curtly, 'I also told Colette she must only talk to people I selected. I don't want this book to be stuffed with scandalous gossip from my enemies. I've seen too many biographies of that sort to want one about myself.'

'Is this the first biography of you?' she asked, surprised, and he nodded, as the waiter came to remove their plates and refill their wine glasses.

Gina dropped her napkin a moment later and, as she bent to retrieve it, saw out of the corner of her eye that Colette was dining with a tall, blond man Gina didn't recognise.

'Who's that with Colette?' she asked Nick who shot a look across the room, then shrugged.

'I can't remember his name, but I've seen him around Barbary Wharf several times this week, on the editorial floor. He's a fast worker, too, obviously, unless he knew Colette before he joined us.'

'You mean you didn't recruit him from one of your other papers?' Gina mocked. Nick's habit of switching staff from one of his European papers to the *Sentinel* to fill vacancies, rather than advertising in the United Kingdom, was not popular with the English members of the *Sentinel*'s staff.

'He must be a new reporter, and you ought to know by now that I don't interfere on that sort of level!' Nick snapped, frowning. 'I only switch senior staff, in top positions, and it is usually just for a year or so. I like to move my top people around; it gives them experience of other situations, other techniques, and helps them build up their languages. Widens their horizons, let's say.'

'But this doesn't apply to English staff?' Gina drily interrupted and he gave her an impatient look.

'Of course it does. I'm starting to move English staff into Europe but it hasn't been easy to begin the process because so few of them spoke other languages, which was why I started by bringing my top European people over here, to hammer the idea home to the English that it was a good idea to be multi-lingual—and it seems to have got through to them; they're learning languages now at a surprising rate. I've been quite impressed with the way the English are finally waking up to the fact that they're Europeans and that English isn't the only language in the world. I'm getting a lot of requests for transfers abroad now, and I am despatching people at a rate of one or two a month, I think.'

'Roz is going to Paris,' agreed Gina, her mouth turning down, and Nick looked at her quickly, his eyes unusually kind.

'You'll miss her.'

'Yes,' she sighed. 'First Hazel, now Roz...I hate changes, people vanishing from my life, it depresses me.'

Nick put his hands across the table and took both of hers firmly, his smile comforting.

'Gina, Europe is shrinking every day, and the process will accelerate over the next decade. Going to visit Roz in Paris, or Hazel, will be no more of a big deal than a trip to the seaside from London at the moment! The flight to Schiphol, for instance, only takes just over an hour, and then you can drive to Middelburg on the autoroute in no time. You could go and come back in a day, at a pinch!'

'We will be going, Roz and I, to see the baby,' she said. 'As soon as we can both manage a couple of days off.'

'Oh, you should stay over there for longer; see something of Hazel, enjoy playing with the baby, explore the place where she's living, find out how Piet's business is coming along...'

She gave him a wry look. 'Play detective for you? Are you hoping Piet will be a flop and have to come back to you?'

Nick flushed and let go of her hands, ran one hand through his black hair in an irritated gesture. 'You think I'm that petty! Well, you're wrong! I'm simply interested—Piet and I have been friends for a long time, I care what happens to him. If I asked him directly he wouldn't tell me if he was doing badly, he's too proud.'

The waiter arrived with their second course and Gina looked blankly at her poached salmon, her mind intent on what Nick had just said.

'I'm sorry, Nick,' she murmured, picking up her fork. 'Of course I understand. I feel the same concern over Roz.' She took a mouthful of fish, sighed. 'This is dreamy. How's your beef?'

'Great,' he said, then, curtly, 'Take a week off to go to Middelburg whenever you like.'

'I've only just come back from one holiday!' protested Gina, laughing.

'Take a long weekend, then!'

'Yes, that's probably what we'll do. Roz thought I could meet her in Paris and she would drive us both to Middelburg.'

'It might well be quicker than going by plane and train,' agreed Nick. 'You spend so much time hanging around airports, waiting for planes, and there are always delays at the other end, not to mention the time it takes to get a hire-car at an airport.'

They had almost finished their meal when someone appeared beside their table, a very tall, very thin man in a smooth city suit, with thick grey hair and blue eyes with wicked mischief in them.

'Good evening, both of you,' he said blandly. 'I tried to catch your eye across the room but you were so absorbed in each other you didn't even notice me.'

Gina looked up with a shock, her face paling. 'Sir Dermot!' She had forgotten all about him tonight. Her new understanding of Nick had pushed everything else to the back of her mind, but now, at the sight of Sir Dermot, it came rushing back: his plans for an attack on Nick, and his reminder to her that she owed old loyalties to her dead husband's family and their newspaper. How could she ever really forget her bitterness over Nick's betrayal of herself and Sir George Tyrrell, the cynicism that had taught her, and the suspicion of Nick's motives? Tonight she had tried, but seeing Sir Dermot again was like opening Pandora's box and being overwhelmed with troubles.

Sir Dermot looked down into her stricken green eyes. 'Yes, I'm back,' he said softly. 'I flew back a few days ago. How are you, Gina? You look very brown—I hear you've been to Egypt; did you have a good time? So did I, in the Caribbean. We must get together as soon as possible and swap holiday snaps.'

Gina felt Nick watching her, his grey eyes hard and narrow as he picked up nuances in Sir Dermot's voice. A wave of guilt and fear swamped her. Nick was right to be suspicious; Sir Dermot was talking about holidays but his eyes were saying something very different. He had come back fit and active again, and ready to fire the opening shots in his war with Caspian International, and he expected her to help him destroy Nick.

CHAPTER NINE

SIR DERMOT rang her next morning, his voice curt and abstracted. 'We must talk, Gina, and soon. How about tonight? Dinner?'

'Nick and I are having dinner at the Mansion House.' She hadn't been looking forward to eating at the Lord Mayor of London's table with much enthusiasm; it would probably be a stuffy evening with a lot of City financiers. But at least it meant she had a good excuse for saying no to Sir Dermot.

'Which evening are you free before the next board meeting?' he then asked, leaving her no option but, reluctantly, to make a definite arrangement with him.

'Wednesday, then,' he said, ringing off, and Gina put down the phone, sighing.

Sophie, who was working opposite her in the office, looked up enquiringly. 'Problems?'

'Who hasn't?'

'Anything I can do to help?'

Gina smiled gratefully. 'Not really, but thanks for offering.' She looked at her watch. 'I must run. I have a meeting with the print workers' committee at eleven.'

They met in the boardroom if it was unoccupied, but this morning Nick had a big meeting scheduled in there with the heads of departments. The print workers were meeting downstairs, in a large room used for recreational purposes usually. It was fitted out with a pool table, darts boards, a television and video player, armchairs, electronic arcade games and a juke box. A cover could be fitted over the pool table so that meetings could be held around it, and when Gina got down there she found the men already seated with folders in front of them.

They all stood up as she came into the room. 'I'm sorry I'm late,' she breathlessly apologised. 'I got held up by a phone call just as I was leaving.'

'That's all right, Mrs Tyrrell, we haven't started yet,' said the committee secretary, shuffling his papers together.

Gina sat down, smiling around the table at the other men who all smiled back. She got on well with them, had managed to talk to each man privately, since these committee meetings had begun, had got each talking about his family, his hobbies, his interests, so that they were already not just faces or names to her, but people she knew personally.

The secretary picked up a typed sheet which lay in front of him. 'Have we all got a copy of this morning's agenda?'

Gina produced her own copy, running her eye down it to refresh her memory. They were still arguing about the time and motion studies Nick had had done, but there were positive issues on the agenda as well. Several interesting suggestions were coming up from this committee, even Nick had to admit that. These men knew their jobs and had sensible ideas on how to improve the way they worked.

'If you're ready to begin, Mrs Tyrrell?' the secretary said and Gina nodded.

'First, I'd like to say that Mr Caspian was very impressed by the proposal put up last month, on the new flexi-time rotas. He accepted all your suggestions and asked me to congratulate you and thank you.'

It wasn't precisely true. Nick hadn't asked her to congratulate them, merely to tell them that he accepted their suggestions. Privately he had told her he was impressed by their efficiency input, but it was entirely Gina's decision to let the men know how pleased Nick was with their ideas. He would probably be afraid they might ask for more money!

On her way to lunch with Roz after the meeting, Gina met Colette Tse outside the Torelli snack bar.

'Did you enjoy your dinner with Nick?' asked Colette with a stiff, cool smile.

'Yes, did you enjoy yours?' Gina would have had to be blind not to pick up the hostility in the other woman's smile. Colette's slanting dark eyes glittered with black feeling. Jealousy? wondered Gina, feeling faintly sick. Was Colette jealous of her over Nick?

'Very much,' the features editor said shortly.

Gina didn't like to walk away, but she couldn't bear the way Colette was looking at her.

She tried to change the atmosphere. 'Who was the blond guy you were with? I didn't recognise him; does he work at Barbary Wharf?'

'Yes.'

Trying to keep smiling, Gina persisted. 'What does he do?'

'Writes features.'

'Oh? What's his name?' Gina knew Colette was trying to humiliate her, but she wasn't giving up yet.

Reluctantly, Colette said, 'Beren Lindell.'

'Unusual! Is he English?'

'Well, he isn't Chinese!' Colette said with a sting in her voice, and Gina pretended to laugh.

'Not with that blond hair and blue eyes! It's just that I don't recognise the name and Nick didn't seem to know him, either.'

Colette's glittering stare focused on her more sharply. 'You and Nick were talking about us?' From her expression Gina knew she had said the wrong thing.

'I asked Nick if he knew him, that's all, and he said he thought he was vaguely familiar. Has he been with us long?' It was heavy going, like trying to walk through glue, but Gina went on trying because she was sure now that Colette felt something pretty serious for Nick, even if he didn't know it, and she was sorry for her. Nick had used her, for his own purposes; to make Gina jealous. It had been a shabby trick, and Gina felt as if it was her fault, too, she shared Nick's guilt: she couldn't blame Colette for hating her. In Colette's shoes she would feel the same.

'A few weeks. He hasn't made his mark yet, but I'm sure he will. He's talented.'

'As well as sexy?' Gina laughed. Colette didn't.

'My interest in him is purely professional,' she said with ice in her voice. 'Excuse me, I'm in a hurry to buy my sandwiches and get back to eat lunch at my desk.' Her eyes contemptuously made it clear that, while she was working while she ate, she suspected Gina was going to be eating a long, leisurely and expensive lunch at Pierre's. And the trouble was, she was right. Gina wasn't working through her lunch-hour. She was meeting a friend to gossip and chatter small talk.

She turned on her heel and went into Torelli's, and Gina walked towards Pierre's, across the plaza, flushed and unhappy.

When Alessa told her that Nick was seeing Colette quite often simply because she was writing a book about the Caspian family, Gina had seen in a flash how Nick had manipulated the situation. Realising she was jealous, he'd gone out of his way to make it look as if he was dating Colette.

When she'd found out he had been playing tricks on her, Gina had been furious, then, as the sting of jealousy faded, it had amused her to plan a revenge. Alessa had promised not to tell her brother she had warned Gina, then Gina only had to wait for him to wave Colette's name in front of her before puncturing his balloon with mockery.

It had been fun to plan, fun to see his face when he realised she knew the truth. It hadn't even entered her head to look at the situation from Colette's angle, but it should have done! She should have realised Colette, too, might have misunderstood Nick's interest in her, might have got hurt. How could Nick have done it? Sometimes she despaired of ever understanding him—understanding any man!

Roz was already waiting for her, and waved from a table in a corner. As Gina walked over there she passed Tom Birny, who grinned up at her.

'Hi!'

She stopped. 'So you're back, too—how are you, Tom? Did you have a good time in Martinique?'

'Terrific! Can't you tell?' He tilted his sunburned face to the light, and Gina laughed.

'Yes, you are brown, aren't you?'

He considered her. 'Where did the big white chief send you? You have a nice tan yourself.'

'Egypt, but I tried to stay out of the sun as much as possible. I've got the wrong sort of colouring for sun-bathing.' She paused, then asked, 'Got any more stuff on the East End Mafia?'

He shook his head. 'Apart from reporting the trial of the guys who tried to get Nick Caspian, no, I think I've more or less milked that story for everything it has got.'

'I'm glad to hear it!'

He grimaced. 'Yes, it certainly stirred things up! But I'm having a problem getting information now—being seen with me isn't popular these days, especially in the East End. People have started to avoid me like the plague!'

Gina gave him a comforting smile. 'Poor Tom. They'll forget about it soon, don't worry.'

'Let's hope you're right.' He didn't seem convinced. 'And in the meantime I'll have to rely on my buddies in the police for every crumb of information, and that won't get me far. They feed me the same stuff they feed every other crime reporter, and I need an inside track.' He looked past her and his face changed. 'Oh, here's my lunch date at last!'

Gina turned to look as he waved to a girl with a very pocket Venus figure, a triangular little face and a head of bubbly golden curls, who had just come into the restaurant and was standing at the door, looking around.

'Sharon! Over here!' Tom called and the girl turned, then did a double-take as she saw Gina with him.

'I must go and join Roz,' Gina tactfully said, not wishing to spoil a budding romance. 'See you around, Tom.'

When she got to the table Roz grinned at her. 'Chatting up Tom Birny? Better not let Nick catch you at it! I must say he's looking good, though; I wish all our men were as hunky as that, and a tan suits him.' She glanced past Gina. 'Who's the teenager he's with?'

'I have no idea,' Gina said, looking through the menu. 'She looks about twelve!'

Gina gave her an amused look, knowing that Roz could be quite tart on the subject of other women, particularly pretty ones. 'Maybe Tom likes his girls young?' She put the menu down, having decided on melon followed by sole, which was what she usually ended up eating at Pierre's. Everything else they offered was too rich and too high in calories.

'Yes,' Roz agreed thoughtfully. 'He's the type, isn't he? He'd like an adoring slave he can pet and protect rather than a grown-up woman who might ask too much of him.'

'Poor Tom, what has he ever done to you?' Gina asked, laughing.

Roz had the grace to laugh back. 'Oh, take no notice, I'm in a ratty mood today. Let's talk about something cheerful—when are we going to make this trip over to see Hazel's baby?'

*   *   *

The following Wednesday Gina arrived for dinner with Sir Dermot at his house and was taken aback to find that the other guests were Philip Slade and his fiancée, Suki, and her parents, Mr and Mrs Tamaki.

'You have met Mr and Mrs Tamaki before, haven't you, Gina?' Sir Dermot smoothly said as they stood up and politely bowed to her.

Bowing back, Gina smiled and said, 'Yes, how do you do? How nice to see you back in London so soon. I hope you are enjoying your visit?'

Mr Tamaki answered in perfect English. He was taller than his wife, and looked as if he could be forty although Gina was pretty sure he was probably closer to fifty years old. He had a strong, fleshless clean-shaven face: direct, arrogant, dark eyes and an air of authority. When he was young he must have been irresistible, thought Gina, even though he did not seem to smile very often.

His wife was wearing a kimono again; a deep blue one this time, with sprays of delicate white plum blossom in the pattern. Did she always wear kimonos? Was that her preference—or her husband's?

Gina sat down in the chair next to her and smiled at her. So far she had not heard Mrs Tamaki say a word, and she wondered if she spoke English.

'Have you been to London many times, Mrs Tamaki?'

Mrs Tamaki smiled shyly, bobbed her head and whispered in a reedy voice, 'My husband he comes, but I stay California. Not liking planes.'

Sympathetically, Gina asked, 'You're afraid to fly? I know how you feel. I was particularly scared after a close friend of mine was hijacked by terrorists while flying to London. Luckily, she wasn't badly injured, but I must say it put me off flying for a long time.'

Mrs Tamaki looked flustered, gave her husband a sidelong look.

'I'm afraid my wife's English is limited,' Mr Tamaki promptly told Gina. 'She couldn't keep up with what you were saying.' He switched to Japanese and his wife listened, her face changing.

She looked back at Gina and nodded, smiling. 'Very bad. Lot of bad things on planes. Hijackers, bombs, fall out of sky... Me, I stay on ground.'

Suki chimed in at that moment. 'My mother keeps trying to learn the language, but she has a bad memory, she forgets most of what she learns, and it doesn't help that she has a Japanese maid, at home, and that most of her friends are Japanese. She doesn't have the incentive to learn that I had, going to school in America.'

'I suppose not.'

'Not if I wanted friends!' Suki said, and Gina gave her a wry look.

'I'm sure you had lots of friends, not to mention admirers. You're so lovely.'

'Thank you,' Suki said, accepting the compliment with a graceful smile. She knew she was beautiful: a fine-boned, slender girl with a glowing golden skin and liquid black eyes, hair like black silk, a perfect red bow of a mouth. She was wearing a cocktail dress Gina envied as soon as she saw it: the same red as her mouth, silky, gleaming like the petals of a poppy.

'After your marriage, are you and Philip going to live here, in London, or go back to the States to live?' Gina glanced at Philip, who sat close beside Suki.

'We plan to stay in London,' Philip said, his eyes meeting Sir Dermot's, then, turning back to Gina, he smiled warmly. 'Actually, that is what we wanted to talk to you about, Gina; I'm glad you raised the question. Ever since we got engaged, Suki's father has been wondering what to give her for a wedding present. As you'll have realised, she's his only daughter, and he wanted to find something very special for her. Suki is ambitious; she wants to have an exciting career here, after our marriage, and the business she really understands is newspapers.' He paused, then went on a little uncertainly,

'What she would like to do is...is...get involved with the *Sentinel*, Gina.'

A little puzzled, Gina smiled at him. 'She wants me to get her a job on the paper?' She turned her eyes to Suki enquiringly. 'What sort of job, exactly?'

Suki laughed lightly. 'A job? No, no, Gina. That isn't what we want.'

'No?' Gina's bewilderment deepened; she looked from one to the other of them, wondering if she had missed part of the conversation. 'Then what are we talking about?'

'The *Sentinel*,' Mr Tamaki's deep, curt voice cut in. 'We are talking about the *Sentinel*.'

Gina stared at him, suddenly beginning to glimpse what they were driving at, her mouth parting on a rough intake of air.

His smile was sardonic. 'We want it.'

She was stricken speechless, turning white, then dark red. Nick had said that Mr Tamaki might be interested in buying the paper, and she had thought he was getting paranoid. But he was right, after all.

Philip said quickly, 'Of course, as you know, I own a small block of shares in the company, and at the moment I hold the balance of power between you and Caspian. I could give the shares to Suki...'

'But it isn't enough,' Suki said coolly, her dark eyes glittering. 'I must have control, which means getting rid of Caspian. It is really very simple, you see, and profitable for you. We want you to sell us your shares and we are prepared to pay the current market value.'

Gina was still working it all out in her head, realising just how Sir Dermot and Philip had been leading her up the garden path with their talk of a board revolt and voting against Nick. All the time they had had this in mind, but they had hidden the truth from her until they thought the time was ripe.

She looked from Suki to her father and saw the likeness between the two of them, saw the smile of satisfaction, of pride in his daughter, in Mr Tamaki's eyes. Suki was made in his image; she was tough and formidable already. What would she be like in ten years' time? Gina felt sorry for Philip. He was marrying an exquisitely lovely woman but inside that beautiful body was a diamond-hard brain and a fierce will. Did he realise that? Or was he blinded by her looks?

'Think about it, Gina,' intervened Sir Dermot, who had discreetly stayed out of the discussion until now. He smiled in that bland way of his, and Gina felt a sudden angry dislike for him.

What was the difference between him and Nick? Sir Dermot had been lying to her, plotting behind her back, just as he had talked her into conspiring behind Nick's back?

Oh, God, she thought with a wild pang—what is the difference between me and him? Between me and Nick? We are all capable of betraying each other, lying and cheating and plotting. She felt sickness in the pit of her stomach.

Sir Dermot smoothly said, 'Gina, I know you've found the past year disturbing. You've gone on doing what you felt you had to do, working alongside Caspian, although it has been a terrible strain for you, fighting him over the way he has changed the paper, out of family loyalty...'

'We respect you for that,' Mr Tamaki intervened seriously, and, looking into his almond-shaped dark eyes, she believed he meant what he was saying. 'Family comes first. With me, too, Mrs Tyrrell. But there is another way for you to stay loyal to your husband's family. For their sake, you want to get rid of Caspian. OK. Sell your shares to us and let us get rid of him for you.'

Sir Dermot nodded. 'Gina, you swore you would make Caspian pay for causing George's death, didn't you? Sell your shares to Tamaki; you'll get your revenge when he realises he has lost control, the way George did.'

Gina slowly shook her head. 'I couldn't sell . . . the old man left those shares to me because he trusted me!'

'He trusted you to do what was best for the *Sentinel*,' Sir Dermot said sharply. 'And that isn't letting Caspian run it! Gina, Gina, I know you're tired of fighting Caspian. That has become increasingly obvious lately, or why were you so reluctant to join us against him? I could see you felt guilty for even discussing it with us! You don't seem able to make up your mind what you want to do, whether you're with him or against him. He's no fool, is he? He has got round you, even though you know what he did to Sir George.'

Scalding colour ran up Gina's face and she looked away, appalled to realise that Sir Dermot had guessed so much about her feelings for Nick.

Watching her intently, Sir Dermot said softly, 'You can't trust him, you know. Don't let him fool you the way he did before. Remember what he did to Sir George. Sell Mr Tamaki your shares, leave it to us to deal with Caspian. Then you can go away and forget about all the *Sentinel*, Caspian, the whole damn business.'

It made a strange sort of sense, and Gina bit her lip, her mind beseiged by a whirl of conflicting ideas. If she sold her shares, it was true, she would be free of a burden she had found increasingly heavy over the year since Sir George Tyrrell had died. She could finally silence her conscience which had been bitterly flaying her in past months for loving Nick, which was a sort of betrayal of her dead husband and his family. She could stop feeling stupidly guilty because she was conspiring with Sir Dermot and Philip Slade against Nick, although why she should feel guilty about that when Nick had been prepared to betray her and Sir George she didn't know! But love wasn't logical. It didn't reason or draw up equations. Love was unpredictable and crazy and she was tired of the pain of loving Nick.

If she sold her shares to Mr Tamaki, she could stop hurting because she was in love with a man she did not trust. Selling her shares would be wiping the slate. Sir Dermot might be talking like a salesman with his foot in the door, but in that, at least, he was right. If she sold her shares, she could go away and start life again, and try to forget.

'Mrs Tyrrell...' Mr Tamaki suddenly said in his deep gruff voice. 'My daughter has set her heart on this, and maybe I spoilt her, but I have always tried to get her what she wanted. Will you sell me your shares, Mrs Tyrrell?'

Gina sighed heavily. 'You can't expect me to decide here and now, Mr Tamaki. I need time to think about it, discuss it with my lawyers, my financial advisers!'

Sir Dermot looked alarmed, stiffening. 'We'd rather you didn't discuss it with anyone, Gina! If Caspian got wind of our plans it could be disastrous.'

'I'll be very discreet, don't worry.'

'All the same——' Sir Dermot began, but Mr Tamaki interrupted him curtly.

'When will you let us know your answer?'

Gina turned her green eyes on him, hesitated. 'A few days?'

He inclined his head. 'Very well. The next board meeting is on Wednesday. Let us know by Monday.'

CHAPTER TEN

GINA had barely walked into the office next morning when Roz rang her. 'I've managed to get this weekend off, starting Friday, so why don't we go to Holland to see Hazel and the baby?'

'This weekend?' repeated Gina, taken by surprise. She looked at her desk calendar. 'It's Thursday today. Go tomorrow, you mean?'

Roz chuckled. 'Yes, idiot! Go tomorrow! Are you free too, or not?'

Gina turned over the pages of her diary. 'Well, there's nothing important, nothing I can't cancel, but...Roz, we haven't booked flights, hotels, anything...' Her voice died away as Nick opened the door and stood there, staring at her. Her heartbeat quickened, her nerves jumped. Just the sight of him did drastic things to her.

'There won't be a problem about getting a flight at this time of year, or a hotel,' said Roz impatiently. 'Do you want to go or not?'

'Of course I want to go!' Gina's voice was low and husky; it made her so nervous to have him watching her like that.

'Go where?' Nick asked tersely.

'Hang on a minute, Roz,' Gina said into the phone, then put the receiver down and moistened her dry lips with the tip of her tongue before telling Nick, 'Holland, to see Hazel and the baby.'

His black brows met, his grey eyes narrowed and hard.

'I know it's short notice, but can I have tomorrow off?' Gina was beginning to see that Roz had offered her a chance to escape for a few days, get away from

Barbary Wharf and London, so that she could think out
her dilemma without the pressure of having Nick or Sir
Dermot or Philip Slade around.

'How long would you be there?'

'Just the weekend; we can be back on Monday.'

He put his hands into his pockets and leaned back
against the door-frame, his long, lean body gracefully
posed. 'I'll fly you there and back,' he offhandedly told
her.

Gina's mouth parted in astonishment, then she realised
what he must have meant. 'You mean you'll send us in
your private jet? Well, that would be kind——'

'No, I mean I will fly you there, myself. Didn't you
know I could fly? No need to look so dubious—I'm
good, even if I say so myself. I've been flying for years,
I can't even remember how many flying hours I've
clocked up. I could earn a living as a pilot if I lost all
my money tomorrow!' He straightened and came over
to the desk, made a peremptory gesture, leaning over
her. 'Give me that phone!'

Gina was abruptly breathless, now that he was so close.
Her hand trembled as he took the phone from her. She
couldn't get away; his body was fencing her in as he
talked to Roz, his face inches from Gina's.

'Roz? Nick here. Look, I want to see my godson, too.
I suggest I fly us all to the nearest airfield to Middelburg.'
He paused, listening to whatever Roz was saying.

Gina lowered her lashes, but from behind them she
watched his hard profile, her body aching with desire.
So close to him she could see every pore in his clean-
shaven skin, his long straight nose, the angle of
cheekbone and jaw, the authority and passion of the
mouth—the razor-edged masculinity which was a
physical expression of Nick's inner power.

From the very beginning she had never been quite sure
how she felt about him because her reactions to him were
so complex and contradictory. There were aspects of

Nick's character she did not approve of or like; there were facets of his nature she found disturbing and frightening, and yet...

And yet when she was near him she always felt this deep, erotic ache inside her, an intense physical awareness she couldn't deny or suppress, and which she could only control by using every effort of energy at her command. Ever since Sir George had died, she had been fighting not only Nick, but her feelings for Nick. The struggle was draining her; she knew she was weakening day by day; it was getting harder and harder to keep him at arm's length, especially now that they had been lovers and Nick had discovered his power over her, the wildness and passion that had flooded out of her as they made love.

'I'll talk to Piet myself today,' he said to Roz, and Gina's heart turned over at the mere sound of that deep voice. Hearing it was like being brushed with black velvet: every hair on the nape of her neck stood up. 'I'll tell him we're coming, make sure we'll be welcome...after all, the baby's only a few days old; Hazel and Piet might prefer us to come later on, when they've had time to get used to having the baby. If he thinks Hazel will want to see us now, I'll ask him to suggest the best local hotel. Then I'll get back to you and let you know what I've fixed up, OK?'

He hung up and Gina prickled with heat as, without straightening, he turned his head and looked into her dilated green eyes.

'I wanted to talk to Roz myself,' she protested, and Nick gave her a mocking little smile.

'Ring her again later. First, I want to talk to you.' He paused, his eyes sharp. 'Where were you last night?'

'What?' Gina felt her face turning scarlet; she couldn't hold his stare and looked away. 'Why?' she hedged.

'I rang you several times,' he said curtly.

She summoned indignation to her rescue, and didn't have to act. He had no right to cross-examine her as if she were on trial. 'Aren't I allowed a private life any more? I was having dinner with someone.'

'Who?' The terse question was like a bullet from a gun and made her flinch, as if it had hurt.

'Don't snap at me like that! I don't have to tell you what I'm doing!'

'Tom Birny?' he asked in the same harsh voice, and the surprise of the question made her laugh.

'No.' She laughed because he was so wrong, so far from the truth. She had been afraid he somehow knew about her dinner with Sir Dermot and Philip Slade and the Tamakis; was aware of the conspiracy against him and her own part in it. Guilt had made her tremble and turn cold, and now she was weak-kneed with relief. Nick always seemed to be able to pick up secrets out of the air, as if he had spies everywhere, or some sort of radar equipment. Gina was half convinced he was in league with the devil, his instincts were so inhumanly accurate.

But not this time, and so her green eyes danced, and Nick glowered at her.

'What's so funny?'

Suddenly Gina sobered, her first relief dissipating and clouds of fear and guilt rolling back. Sooner or later Nick was going to find out what had been happening behind his back, and her heart failed her at the thought of how he would look at her.

'Nothing,' she said huskily. 'Nothing is funny at all.' Then before he could demand to know what she was talking about, she hurriedly asked, 'Exactly where is Middelburg?'

'It's in the southern Netherlands, close to the North Sea coast and the river Schelde's estuary, not far from Vlissingen ... the English used to call that Flushing. Middelburg isn't far from the Belgium border, either. If we had more time we could drive to Harwich on the east coast and take a car ferry across to the Hague then drive to Middelburg, but as we only have a weekend we'll fly and pick up a hire car.' He looked at his watch. 'I'll ring Piet now. Ask one of those girls to bring me a coffee, will you?'

He walked away into his own office and Gina watched him with an ache of longing. He would never forgive her if she sold her shares to Mr Tamaki. Yet if she didn't, if she turned her back on everything the Tyrrells had meant, if she didn't keep her oath to avenge Sir George, how could she forgive herself? Whichever way you looked at it there was no future for her and Nick. Too much lay between them.

Even as she told herself that, she felt a wild pang of grief, of yearning, and then a darkness filled her head, a cloudy anger and frustration. It wasn't fair! Why was her life in such a tangle? What had she ever done to deserve it? Except fall in love with the wrong man?

The shops stayed open until eight in the evening on Thursdays, so Gina and Roz went straight from work to the West End to buy presents for Hazel and the baby to take with them next day. They found what they wanted quite quickly: fashionable baby clothes from Mothercare for baby Nicholas, then Gina bought Hazel a bottle of Chanel, a perfume she knew Hazel liked, while Roz bought her a pair of very pretty earrings.

They arrived at Middelburg on the Friday afternoon, driving through green and lovely countryside which shone tranquilly under a delicate lavender-blue winter sky. There was a shimmer about the landscape; the reflections of sky in water everywhere, it seemed. They were driving on roads built over dikes and estuaries of rivers—they had been built, Nick told them, after terrible storms overwhelmed this whole coastline in the 1950s and the North Sea flooded in over the land, destroying everything in its path and killing several thousand people.

'It looks so calm and peaceful,' said Gina incredulously, staring across the low-lying polder fields with their green willows and hazels, their grazing cows, windmills and little farm houses.

'Today, yes,' said Nick. 'But it isn't wise to underestimate the sea.' He shot her a sideways glance through his black lashes, his mouth curling mockingly. 'Or any natural force.'

A little flush crept up her face. He didn't have to keep dropping these oblique, provocative hints. She was only too well aware of the risks one took in fighting the natural force Nick meant. She knew love was as elemental as the sea and, potentially, just as destructive. She crossly pretended to be unaware of his watchful gaze, keeping her eyes fixed on the Zeeland countryside through which they drove.

'It's an odd name...Zeeland...' she thought aloud, and Nick laughed.

'Obvious what it means—sea-land, reclaimed from the sea!'

'Oh! Of course.' She hadn't thought of that.

Roz was in the back of the hire car Nick had collected after they landed at Rotterdam airport, looking exhausted, not surprisingly. It had surprised Gina to see her turn pale as the plane took off from London, and to realise that Roz was very nervous once they were in the air. Puzzled, Gina had been tactless enough to mention it and Roz had grimly admitted that ever since the hijacking incident last year she had been scared of flying.

'Why didn't you say something?' Gina had asked, horrified, and Roz had shrugged.

'My job means I have to fly all the time, I just have to put up with being scared, and I expect it will wear off one day.' Gina had been dumb with admiration: Roz had such depths of tenacity.

'How much further is it to Middelburg?' Roz asked now in a low, tired voice.

'We should be there any time,' said Nick, shooting her a concerned glance in his driving mirror. Gina saw it, and realised that although she hadn't mentioned Roz's fear to Nick he knew about it, or guessed, at least. 'Not long now,' he said quite gently, and not for the first time Gina thought how kind he could be, unexpectedly, what good instincts he had about people. He picked up their feelings out of the air.

Somehow, though, he managed to miss the turning to Piet and Hazel's home, and they found themselves driving into the medieval centre of the little town, with its twelfth-century abbey, clustered church spires and carefully preserved old houses dominated by a tower which must have been well over a thousand feet high. The complicated traffic system meant that Nick took some time to fight his way out again and got into something of a temper before they managed to find the right road.

Hazel and Piet lived just outside the town, in a weather-worn old stone building which Hazel had said had once been a farm barn. Piet had redesigned and modernised it, turning it into a gracious and very individual home and workplace, because their firm would operate from here as well.

Piet came out to meet them while they were parking on his driveway, hugged both girls and shook hands with Nick, obviously delighted to see them all, his blond hair gleaming smoothly in the wintry light and his blue eyes intensely bright.

'It's so good to see you here! Hazel will be so happy, she still feels a little lost, I think, but now the baby has come she will be too busy to feel lonely any more.'

Gina gave him a quick, anxious look. Had Hazel been feeling lost and lonely since she moved here? Piet met her eyes and smiled reassuringly.

'Don't look so worried, Gina! It was natural. Holland is a strange country to her. But she will love it here. Hazel may have been born in England but she has a Dutch character.'

Gina giggled.

He winked at her. 'Yes, it is true. She has all the Dutch virtues: she is hard-working and very orderly, she is fastidious and careful, she is honest...'

'Stop praising your own people and let's get inside,' growled Nick. 'I'm dying for a drink.'

'Of course, what am I thinking of? Come in, come in...you must be cold after your drive from Rotterdam—did it take long?'

'We would have been here hours ago if Nick hadn't tried to drive into Middelburg and gone round and round their one-way street system trying to get out again!' Gina said, and Piet laughed.

'You didn't, Nick? You should have parked in the public car park by the canal; it's huge, takes hundreds of cars, then you just walk across the canal into town. Middelburg's streets are far too narrow for cars.'

'So I noticed,' Nick said acidly. 'But I didn't intend to drive into Middelburg. I lost my way arguing with Gina.'

'Oh, it's my fault, is it?' she said. 'I might have known it would be.'

Tactfully, Roz said, 'But Middelburg is a fascinating town. I'm glad I saw some of it; I'd like to walk around the centre while I'm here.'

'You must, there's a lot to see,' Piet agreed. 'They completely reconstructed the medieval centre after the war—some of it was badly damaged. But do you know, you can still see the tide-marks on some of the house walls in town, where the Allies breached the dykes and flooded Middelburg during the last days of the war in Europe.'

'Oh, what a terrible thing to do!' said Gina, shocked.

'Well, some of us thought so!' said Piet as she followed him through the Gothic arch of the front door into a dark-beamed, vaulted hallway. 'This is all the old barn,' he explained to Nick, who was staring around in interest. 'I've added new buildings at the rear and side.'

'Where are Hazel and the baby?' Gina asked. 'I'm dying to see them.'

Piet smiled at her warmly. 'Upstairs; go on up, you two girls, while I get Nick his drink. Hazel is up and about now, but the doctor wants her to get plenty of rest during the day so I'm making her stay in bed as much as possible. It isn't easy. You know how stubborn she can be!'

They found Hazel in bed, in a pretty cream and pink bedroom flooded with light from two high, arched windows. She heard them coming up the stairs and called out to them. 'In here, Gina!'

They pushed open the first door and there she was, sitting up against banked pillows, in a warmly comfortable Victorian-style pink nightdress, with a high, frilled neck and long sleeves, a lacy white shawl around her shoulders, her hair brushed and shining, her eyes bright as she beamed at them.

'Oh, I'm so glad to see you!'

Gina hugged her. 'You look terrific! Being a mum suits you!' Then she looked eagerly at the small, polished mahogany swinging cradle beside the bed. 'Is he in there?' The cradle was hung with gauzy white curtains which were pulled together, but Gina could see a little bump under the white covers.

'Yes, asleep,' said Hazel, leaning over to pull one of the curtains aside.

On tiptoe Gina and Roz peered down at the tiny head, pink scalp dusted with blond hairs.

'I wasn't expecting it to be so small, it looks like a doll,' said Roz, and it was true, there was a waxy look to the baby's profile, the eyes closed, the mouth pursed, the cheeks pale in sleep.

'Not it! He!' Hazel indignantly reminded. 'We're calling him Nicholas. Nicky, for short, so that we don't confuse him with Nick Caspian.'

'He's beautiful,' said Gina, feeling a wrench of envy in her stomach. 'He's going to be blond like his daddy; isn't he lucky?' She badly wanted to pick the baby up, hold him, feel the breathing warmth of the tiny body close to her. 'I can't wait to give him a cuddle!' she said, and Hazel smiled at her.

Roz gave them both a wry, amused look. 'What is it that makes a woman feel broody whenever she sees a newborn baby?'

'Instinct,' said Gina softly.

'Hormones,' Roz said with her usual cynicism. 'Women are the victims of their own chemistry.'

Hazel and Gina looked at each other and Hazel winked. 'Oh, I do miss you, you know,' Gina broke out. 'Even though Sophie is very good at the job, it isn't the same as having you there to chat to every day.'

'She's getting on well, though, is she? I'm glad. I thought she might be too nervous of Nick. I mean, Guy Faulkner isn't as tough a nut as Nick can be! I've always thought I'd hate to cross Nick; I suspect he could be quite vindictive.'

Gina shivered.

'Are you cold?' asked Hazel, surprised. 'The central heating is on—I thought the house was too warm, myself.'

'It is warm,' said Gina, and Hazel gave her a searching look.

'Someone walk over your grave?'

Gina shivered again. 'I hate that expression!'

The truth was, she was afraid Hazel was right—Nick would be vindictive and unforgiving if he thought she had betrayed him. If she sold her shares to Mr Tamaki...

'Well,' said Hazel, tactfully changing the subject as she saw that Gina was upset and unwilling to talk about it. 'While you're here we'll be able to gossip away for hours. You can tell me all the Barbary Wharf scandal. I only wish you were staying longer. Must you go back on Monday?'

'There's a board meeting on Wednesday and we have to be back for that!' Nick's deep voice said from the door. Gina started violently, her nerves leaping. How long had he been there? She tried to remember what they had been saying, alarmed by the idea of Nick listening to her when she didn't know he was there.

Hazel looked pleased to see him. 'Hello! I'd wondered where you had got to! I suppose you and Piet have been drinking downstairs?'

'Having a baby is a good excuse for a few drinks,' Nick agreed, amused.

'So he keeps telling me! Well, don't stand out there, come in—I want to thank you for flying Gina and Roz here to see us, I was dying to show off my baby to them both.'

'It was a pleasure. I was keen to come and see my godson.'

He walked towards them, immediately making the room seem smaller with the dynamism of his presence because that tall, lean body dominated every room he entered. 'You look wonderful, Hazel—motherhood suits you!' He was carrying the basket which held the gifts they had brought with them. 'You forgot these!' he told Gina and Roz.

Hazel was delighted with her presents, unwrapping them with the eagerness of a child, exclaiming and admiring, but, Gina noticed with fond amusement, neatly folding the wrapping paper and tags. No wonder Piet said Hazel fitted in well in his country! She had always had a passion for order, as her new home testified. Everything in this house was in apple-pie order.

When she had finished thanking Gina and Roz, Nick suddenly dropped on the bed cover a small envelope with 'Hazel' written on it in his dramatically sprawling handwriting. It rattled as it fell, and, puzzled, Hazel looked up at him.

'What's this?'

'Open it and find out!'

She picked up a paperknife lying on her beside table and slit the envelope. Out fell a set of keys on a gold keyring which carried her initial.

Mystified, Hazel picked them up. 'I don't understand . . . what are they for?'

Nick grinned at her. 'They're car keys, of course! I checked with Piet before I bought it, to make sure you drove.'

'Car keys?' she gasped incredulously, eyes wide, and Roz and Gina exchanged startled looks.

'For a car, which I've ordered from your local dealer,' he said offhandedly, yet with a little red streak along his cheekbones as if he was uncomfortable. 'I chose it in white, it seemed appropriate, but if you would prefer another colour the dealer will change it. This model is a hatchback estate car, with lots of room at the the the back for prams and shopping and so on! All you have to do is ring the dealer and tell him when you want it delivered and he'll drive it over here.'

'I . . . I don't know what to say!' Hazel was pale with excitement, trembling a little.

'No need to say anything. I wanted to get you something you really needed, and I remembered Piet saying something about looking out for a good second-hand car for you because you hadn't got a car at the moment, and, living out here in the country you were going to need one once the baby arrived. So that settled my present problem.'

'I'm stunned, it's so generous, so...thank you, Nick, it's the best present you could possibly have given me and I——'

At that instant the baby chose to wake up and start to cry in a wailing complaint. 'Oh, dear,' said Hazel, distracted, turning towards the cradle, but before she could lean down Nick was there. Gina watched disbelievingly as he picked the baby up as if used to handling babies every day, one hand under the blue terry-towelling baby-gro the baby wore, the other hand casually supporting the floppy little blond head. He held the baby out in front of him at arm's length and made a cheerful clucking noise.

The baby's eyes opened wide; he stopped crying and stared up into Nick's face.

'Hello, Nicky, I'm your godfather,' Nick said, stroking the baby's flushed cheek with one long index finger.

Watching the tenderness in his face, the smile in his grey eyes, the warm curve of his mouth, Gina felt her heart turn over. He was the most complicated and bewildering human being she had ever met: a mass of contradictions and dangerously easy to love.

During the weekend she managed to get Hazel alone for an hour, and tell her the quandary she was in over her shares in the *Sentinel*. Hazel listened, startled, watching her closely.

'I can see it would lift some of the weight from your shoulders to be free of those shares, Gina,' she said later. 'I think you're being crippled by the responsibility of being the last Tyrrell and feeling you have to make Nick pay for taking the company away from Sir George. If you no longer own the shares you'll be free of all that.'

'Yes,' said Gina, thinking, And then maybe I'll finally find out whether or not Nick loves me—or is after my shares in the company? There were many very powerful reasons why she should sell to the Tamakis, it seemed.

Piet was eager to show Nick the site of a new church he had just been commissioned to design, and Gina and Roz were having so much fun helping Hazel with the housework and the baby that in the end it was Monday evening before they flew back to London in Nick's private jet.

Roz was still nervous of flying: she put on headphones to drown out the sound of the engines, and shut her eyes and tried to pretend she wasn't in the air at all. Gina sat beside Nick: watching him handle the controls, his strong, sinewy hands deft and confident. She wished she could confide her quandary to him as she had to Hazel, and ask him what she ought to do. But, of course, he was the root of her dilemma and he was the last person she could talk to. Yet even considering asking him made her realise how much she had come to trust him.

Nick suddenly turned to look at her, pushing back the black leather headphones covering his ears.

'How would you like to learn to fly?'

'Me?' Her green eyes lit up. 'I'd love to! But isn't it difficult?'

'Anyone can learn how to fly,' he murmured. 'So long as you never forget what a powerful machine you're dealing with.'

He put out a hand, took one of hers and carried it over to the controls, held it there so that she felt the power and energy pushing and vibrating against her palm. Nick's black lashes flicked sideways; she saw the mocking grey gleam of his eyes.

'I'd enjoy teaching you. Any time.'

Pink ran up Gina's cheeks; she picked up the double meaning but pretended to take his words at face value. 'Are you qualified?'

'Eminently,' he drawled.

'You've taught other people?'

'A few,' he said, mouth twisting. 'And I've never had any complaints. Once they start, they love it and want to do it all the time.'

Gina pulled her hand free. 'Well, thanks for the offer, it's very thoughtful of you,' she drily said. 'But I'm not sure I have the right temperament for such an exciting hobby.'

'Oh, I think you'd be a very good pupil!'

Her flush deepened. 'And I don't know that I'm reassured by hearing that you've had so many other pupils in the past.'

'That past was a long time ago, Gina,' Nick said soberly, frowning at her.

She stared out into the pale blue winter sky through which they flew and didn't answer.

'There hasn't been anyone but you since we met!' he insisted.

She turned an anguished face to him, her voice shaking. 'How can I believe you? How can I ever believe you? You've lied to me before.'

He put out his hand to her again but she pushed him away.

'No, Nick. Leave me alone.'

'Gina, for God's sake——' he broke out in a low, harsh voice, then he stopped short and she heard him breathing raggedly for a moment. 'This isn't the time or the place,' he said at last. 'But we must talk, Gina. I'm going crazy waiting for you to make up your mind whether you'll have me or not. I won't wait much longer.'

She didn't reply, biting down on her lower lip until it bled. Nick wouldn't have to wait much longer. Suddenly she knew what she must do: the only course of action left open to her. Nick was right—the situation between them had dragged on far too long, and unless she did something desperate it would continue to be impossible for her to be sure about him. She would sell her shares to Mr Tamaki, and then she would find out whether

Nick loved her, or whether he merely wanted her as a passive partner in his United Kingdom operation.

When she got back to her apartment she found the answering machine full of calls from Sir Dermot and Philip Slade, demanding to know what she had decided and asking her to return their calls. Gina was too tired to do so; she had a bath and went to bed in a state of depression.

She left for the office early next day, and spent most of the morning in a long meeting with the accountants and the auditors who were still working on last year's company figures. It was a singularly tedious meeting, but necessary. Gina had to force herself to stay alert and interested in what was said.

She had lunch with Nick in the boardroom with the auditors: smoked salmon followed by thinly sliced grilled steak served with salad, then Stilton cheese and biscuits. They ended with coffee and then went back to the second half of the discussions, and this time Nick joined them too.

Gina caught herself clock-watching towards the end of the afternoon, and was intensely relieved when the meeting broke up just before five.

When she returned to her own office, Sophie told her, 'You've had calls from a number of people; some I dealt with, but everyone on this list has been ringing all day; they say it's urgent that you call them back before the board meeting tomorrow!'

Gina guessed the names which would be on the list before she read them. She took the paper from Sophie, sighing. Nick came up behind her silently, while she was looking at the sheet of paper, and before she realised he was there began to read over her shoulder.

'Gaskell, Slade, Suki Tamaki . . . why are they so desperate to talk to you before the board meeting, Gina?'

She spun, her face burning. Sophie discreetly slid out of the room, murmuring something about getting ready to go home.

'Well? What's this all about, Gina?' demanded Nick, watching her.

She swallowed and then, feeling like a trapped animal, muttered, 'Mr Tamaki wants to buy my shares in the *Sentinel*.'

Nick drew an audible breath. 'So I was right. I knew this was coming; I told you so! I kept picking up vibes from Gaskell, Slade, all of them—I knew there was some sort of conspiracy going on, and I guessed Tamaki was behind it. It was the only logical conclusion.'

Gina's hot colour had ebbed; she was white now, her skin icy.

Nick's eyes hardened, darkened. He looked at her as if she was a stranger; with anger and hostility. There was no love in his face now.

'He's waiting for his answer, is he? That's what all the urgency is about? He needs to know before tomorrow's board meeting.' He waited but she couldn't make a sound—her throat was too dry, her mouth full of the ashes of grief and pain. 'So, what are you going to tell him, Gina?' Nick asked at last in a flat, cold voice. 'Yes, or no?'

'Yes,' she whispered then. 'I shall sell.'

CHAPTER ELEVEN

GINA was too disturbed to go home that evening. She knew that if she was in the apartment Sir Dermot, or Philip, would undoubtedly ring her or even come round in person and demand to see her and although she had decided to sell her shares she couldn't yet face talking about it, being rushed into signing anything. She couldn't bear to be alone, either, so she didn't go to a hotel—her first thought. Instead, she rang Roz who without asking any questions said that of course she could stay the night, she was welcome any time and could borrow a nightie so that she needn't even go home for one.

Daniel tactfully left the two women alone in the sitting-room of the little apartment he shared with Roz, while he stayed in the kitchen, cooking dinner for them all, playing passionate Puccini at a deafening volume, and drinking, as Roz drily guessed, the rest of the wine he had opened to use in the succulent *blanquette de volaille* he was cooking. Daniel knew it was one of Gina's favourite dishes: slices of chicken simmered with onions, mushrooms, white wine, yolk of egg and cream. It made a good dish for guests because it could be stretched easily with more mushrooms, more wine, more boiled rice.

'And Nick was beside himself with rage, I suppose?' Roz suggested, as Gina absently drank some of her glass of kir, the liqueur rich and yet sharp on the palate.

Gina laughed wildly. 'Understatement. I thought for a minute he was going to hit me.'

'But he didn't?'

'It was a struggle but he managed to control himself.'

Roz gave her an impatient look. 'Gina, what did you expect? You know he would buy those shares from you. Why sell them to Tamaki, knowing Nick will lose control?'

'That's what he said. He offered double whatever Tamaki is offering.'

Roz whistled. 'You're kidding? That means it is deadly serious; he's afraid of Tamaki, he thinks he will lose the paper.'

Gina nodded bleakly and finished her drink. The wine and *crème de cassis* circulated in her veins, giving her a little more warmth, but she still felt weary and depressed and very cold.

'I wish you would change your mind,' Roz said suddenly. 'You know I'm pretty neutral about Nick Caspian, I've known him a long time and he can be an utter bastard, but he is a good newspaper man, and I have to admit on the whole I think he has been good for the *Sentinel*——'

'Oh, come on, Roz, I've heard you call him every name under the sun for what he has done to the paper!'

Roz grimaced. 'I didn't realise what he had in mind at first, but since I've seen his plans in operation I've been impressed. I'm all in favour of the Europeanisation of the paper; he's giving the editorial staff more opportunities than they ever had before. I'm sorry, Gina, but I have to be honest. Under the Tyrrells, the paper was static and...well, myopic about anything that wasn't solidly British...'

Gina stirred, scowling. 'They were a product of their time and place; what could you expect?'

'True, and they had no idea what being a European meant. You probably don't realise how infuriating that insularity can be! Oh, I know all nations have their own version of it. Watch a French TV newscast. They're only interested in French news. I know. But it is time we changed all that, and Caspian is doing his best to see it does change. Look at the way staff can move freely from one Caspian paper to another, get experience of the way other countries see issues, look at the world from other angles, work with other nationalities! Then, in due course, they can bring that expertise back to Britain and build on it to make the *Sentinel* a truly great paper with a strong European identity and an understanding of what Europe really means.'

'You've been listening to Nick!' Gina accused, and from the doorway, Daniel gave Roz a slow handclap.

'Standing for parliament, *chérie*?' he grinned.

She turned, laughing back at him. 'Was I being pompous? Maybe I was, but I meant every word, and, if I am quoting Nick, so what? I agreed with everything he said, and I think he's brilliant.'

'"Jealous lover shoots newspaper magnate",' said Daniel in deep, hollow tones.

Roz giggled. 'Never mind the jokes. Is dinner ready?'

'Spoken like a true Frenchwoman. The way to her heart is through her stomach. 'Yes, *chèrie*, dinner is ready. Now, stop bullying Gina, and come and eat before my masterpiece gets cold.'

Gina didn't sleep much that night. She slid in and out of confusing dreams, her brow feverish, her hands and feet ice-cold. In the morning she drove to the office a little later than usual, with Roz and Daniel, whose working hours were rather different, on editorial, from those of the executive and administrative staff.

When she got to the boardroom she found most of the directors already gathered there. All eyes flashed to her as she entered the room: without looking in their direction she knew that Philip and Terry Calvert were standing in a group with Sir Dermot and she felt their eyes fix on her, then Sir Dermot descended on her, his face tense, flushed with anger.

'Gina, what the hell have you been playing at?' he began in a whisper, grabbing her arm in tight fingers.

'I've been ringing you ever since Monday; you must have got my messages—why haven't you replied? I don't know what sort of game you think this is, but there's no time for any of this cat and mouse stuff. We have to know. Will you sell or——?' He broke off as Nick walked into the room behind him.

Nick turned hard, sardonic eyes on them, nodding. 'Sir Dermot! How are you feeling this morning? Ready for the battle?'

Sir Dermot's lips stretched whitely in a bitter smile. 'I hope we're going to have a very interesting meeting, anyway, Nick, with a few surprises on the agenda.'

'Nothing ever takes me by surprise, Dermot,' Nick drawled. 'Shall we all sit down?' He waved Gina forward and walked beside her, like a gaoler with a prisoner, to the head of the long, polished table while from the wall the portrait of his father watched them all with a cynical smile.

Gina stared down at the gleaming surface of the table, seeing her own reflection there. Nick called the meeting to order, everyone took their places and then Sophie, sitting behind Nick, read out the minutes of the last meeting in her cool, careful voice.

Then Nick picked up the typed agenda lying in front of him. 'I see that the first matter we're discussing is the interim auditor's report,' he murmured. 'I assume you've all had time to study it.'

There was a rustle as people opened the white folder containing the typed report. Gina automatically opened her copy too. Philip Slade was sitting beside her: he suddenly pushed something into her hand and Gina reluctantly unfolded the piece of paper. As she had expected it was a scrawled note from Sir Dermot. 'Yes or no?' it said. She stared down at it blindly.

The discussions on the auditor's interim report were in full flood. There was a wide range of points of view, but a good many of the people round the table were more interested in watching Gina and waiting for her to give Sir Dermot some sort of answer.

'As this is only an interim report and we haven't had much time to absorb the contents I suggest we either debate this another day or wait until we get the final report,' said Nick, perfectly conscious of what was really going on in the boardroom, but maintaining a cool, cynical front which made him oddly reminiscent of his father, in spite of the fact that they were not otherwise much alike. 'Shall we take a vote on it?' he ended. 'Show of hands? In favour of waiting for the final report?'

Hands went up. Sophie counted them. Nick waited, then said, 'And in favour of debating the interim report at the next board meeting?'

Another flurry of hands. Sophie counted them. Nick asked politely, 'Gina? Are you abstaining?'

Gina swallowed, then she looked up. 'Will you buy my shares?' she asked Nick.

There was an intake of breath around the table. 'Gina, for God's sake!' Philip broke out, shaking and turning white.

Sir Dermot didn't say a word, he just sat there staring at her, his face like stone, his eyes reptilian.

Gina kept her eyes on Nick. He was staring back at her, no expression in his face.

'This isn't the place for a discussion of this sort,' he said at last, his voice steady and calm.

'No, it certainly isn't,' Philip hurriedly said, his hands trembling on the table. He slid them both down out of sight, realising it.

Nick paused, added in the same casual voice, 'But I suppose the circumstances are exceptional, and, since everything we say in this meeting will be on record, yes, I will buy your shares, at the price I offered you last night.'

There was silence. Sir Dermot got up, his eyes spitting rage at Gina. 'There's only one word for what you've done,' he said viciously. 'Treachery. You just betrayed the Tyrrells, for Caspian's dirty money—and maybe that was always what you wanted, right from the beginning. I suppose that's why you married James—for his grand-father's money. Well, I thank God the old man isn't here today to see what you've done. He must be turning in his grave, you treacherous little bitch.'

White and trembling, Gina didn't answer. Nick was on his feet though, dark-faced and grim, growling in his throat like an angry dog. 'That's enough, Gaskell. I'd knock you down if you were my own age. Get out of here, though, before I have you thrown out.'

Sir Dermot stared at him, his hands clenched, then shrugged, turned and walked out of the room, without another word, followed a second later by Philip, who knocked over his chair as he rose in a hurry, amid a buzz of whispered comment from the other directors, who were watching all this like spectators at a circus.

'Shall we get on with the morning's business?' Nick coolly asked, but Gina did not have his nerve. She got up and fled, afraid that any minute she would burst into tears in front of them all.

She got her coat and went for a walk along the river, watching hungry gulls fighting over a piece of bread, watching cold winter sunlight moving over the surface of the water, the bare black boughs of trees in the Embankment gardens, the pale stone of bridges and churches. All around her lay London, city of seven million people, roaring with traffic; yet in the garden there was a strange, hushed quiet and Gina felt lonely and lost.

What was she going to do now? She would no longer be a major shareholder in the company, which meant she lost her place on the board of directors, and any power she had once had.

She couldn't stay in her job, either, she realised. She couldn't go on working for Nick, seeing him every day.

She would have to leave—but at that moment she couldn't imagine a future so different from the past, a future without Nick. It was like looking into an abyss. She felt a sort of vertigo, everything began to swim dazedly in front of her, she had to stop walking, and leant on a bench, sick and shivering.

'Gina, what's wrong?'

Nick's voice was like an electric shock. Her head came up, she swung round, her green eyes enormous in her white face.

'Go away, Nick,' she whispered through dry lips. 'Please. I have to be alone for a while.'

'It's cold out here, and you haven't even buttoned up your coat!' he scolded her, and began doing up the two top buttons as if she were a child.

She shifted fretfully. 'The meeting can't be over already; what are you doing out here?'

'Looking for you.' Nick framed her cold face in his hands, his palms warm against her skin. 'I was worried when you weren't in the office, then I saw you from the window. What are you doing out here? That wind is like a knife.'

She gave him a bitter look. 'You've got what you've always wanted—complete control. There's no need to go on pretending you care what happens to me.'

He looked down into her eyes, his face curiously taut. For a moment she thought he wasn't going to say anything, was going to turn and walk away, and it was like dying inside, the pain was intolerable.

Then he asked in a low, husky voice, 'Will you marry me, Gina?' and the pain grew worse, eating away at her until she could have screamed with it because he was only asking because he felt he should, after she had saved his control of the *Sentinel* by handing him her shares. She knew by now how strong a sense of loyalty and duty Nick had. She knew why he was asking her to marry him, and it was not because he loved her.

'No,' she whispered. 'No. No.'

'Darling, stop it,' said Nick harshly, shaking her.

'No, you stop it,' she shouted, pushing at his broad shoulders in an angry effort to escape. 'Don't you manhandle me! Stop pestering me, go away and leave me alone!'

Nick was flushed now, his eyes dark with temper. 'What do I have to do to prove I love you, you obstinate, stupid woman?' he snapped back at her. 'I've tried over the last year, God knows. Short of lying down and letting you walk all over me, I've done everything I could think of to show you how I felt about you, but all I get is a slap in the face every time I see you.'

'That's right, start bullying me now! I knew you would, sooner or later, that's your usual technique if you can't get your own way.'

Nick stared at her angry mouth and suddenly something in the glitter of his grey eyes, in the tension of his bone-structure, made her feel breathless and weak.

'There's only one way to shut you up, isn't there?' he said hoarsely, and Gina's heart stopped.

It started again a second later as Nick's head swooped down towards her.

'Don't,' she wailed, twisting in his grip.

His mouth hunted insistently over her face as she wriggled and fought. 'You drive me crazy, you stubborn little madam,' Nick muttered into her skin, then she felt his hand behind her, moving into the small of her back.

'Oh,' she gasped as it pulled her forward; so hard that she was slammed right into him. Before she could recover, Nick's other hand closed on her nape and held her head where he wanted it until his searching mouth had found hers, and Gina was lost, dizzy with pleasure and pain and a terrible, consuming desire.

She gave herself up to that kiss without holding anything back, her body weakly yielding, her arms going round him to hold him closer. The heat and tenderness in his lips sent the blood singing into her ears, made her shudder in helpless response.

Nick suddenly pulled back his head, breathing thickly, his skin hot and dark red. Gina reluctantly opened her eyes and met his glittering, passionate stare.

'For the hundredth time, Gina. I love you. Will you marry me?'

'I don't know, I can't think when you kiss me,' she moaned, and Nick laughed angrily.

'Maybe I'd better just keep on kissing you until I get you to the altar!'

'It isn't funny, Nick!'

'No, it isn't, but with you I either have to laugh or get so mad I want to smash things!' He glanced up towards the dark bulk of the complex, frowning. 'And meanwhile, anyone can see us from Barbary Wharf, damn it. We've probably got an audience of thousands! Come on, I'm taking you home where we can at least talk this out alone.'

He slid an arm round her shoulders, but Gina resisted his attempt to get her to walk with him.

'No, Nick. I'm not going home with you; do you think I don't know your methods of persuasion? Don't worry, I'll keep my word and sell you the Tyrrell shares. I'm not going to change my mind. You don't have to keep up this charade; you've won.'

His face tightened, his eyes flashed. 'Forget the shares. Forget the *Sentinel*. Forget the bloody Tyrrells. Listen to me, Gina.' He paused, said the words singly, one by one, with angry force. '*I love you.*'

She stared up at him, trembling, wanting so much to believe it that she was terrified.

Nick waited, watching her. The colour drained out of his face slowly and left it white. He let go of her and his hands fell by his side, empty and open.

'I'll give you the shares back,' he said. 'All of them, including the ones I bought from Sir George. Take the

Sentinel, you can have it, the damned thing has ruined my life.'

He turned and began to walk away and Gina stared disbelievingly after him.

Then she began to run. 'Nick! Wait...Nick...I love you...'

He turned and held out his arms, caught her and held her, tightly; her head against his shoulder and his face buried in her hair.

Later, in her apartment, Nick said huskily, 'That was the biggest gamble I ever took.'

Lying on the sofa in his arms, Gina smiled up at him wryly. 'Did you mean it, would you have handed me back all the shares of the *Sentinel*, or was it just another of your little games?'

'You still don't trust me?' For a second his eyes were dark, and her heart turned over.

'Yes,' she told him at once, knowing it was true at last. 'I trust you, Nick.'

He sighed but smiled, his mouth wry. 'I wonder? Well, give me a chance to prove you can, that's all I need. I'm still feeling as if I'd been knocked off my feet. It has been quite a day so far and we haven't even had lunch!'

She giggled. 'Are you hungry?'

His eyes were passionate. 'Not for food.'

She blushed and Nick laughed softly, in his throat, then caressed her cheek, her throat, with a hand that shook slightly. 'I want you badly, Gina, I always have; it got worse, day by day, until it was almost unbearable and I was ready to do anything to get you. That's why I risked my whole UK operation. You know, when I was walking away, out there on the river path, I felt like someone on his way to the scaffold, I didn't have a clue how you'd react, whether I'd just lost you or whether it had been the right thing to do, whether you would see then that I did love you. The idea of never seeing you again made me want to howl like a dog...and then you came after me and everything changed in a second...'

'You won your gamble, you mean!' she teased him. 'What would you have done if you had lost?'

'God knows. Pulled out of the UK until I found another paper to buy? I just knew I didn't want the *Sentinel* if it meant I lost you. By the way, I still mean to give you all those shares. They'll be my wedding present. I'll stand down as chairman of the board and you'll take over. You are going to be a powerful woman, Gina.' He watched her lazily through his lashes, smiling. 'How does it feel?'

'You can't be serious! Me...chairman...?' She was stunned.

Nick laughed, then sobered. 'Of course I'm serious, I've been nursing you along for the job ever since I took over. You weren't ready for it a year ago; you are now. I've been impressed with the way you've handled yourself with the print workers, the auditors, at board meetings...you're going to be good at the job, Gina. I shall be able to focus on my next European target, knowing that the *Sentinel* is in good hands. I've spent far too much of my time in London over the last year.'

Gina watched him anxiously, her face tense. 'Does all this mean that we won't see much of you in London from now on?'

Nick shot her a look, his eyes gleaming. 'Are you asking me if I'm going to be an absentee husband? No, darling, you are going to see a lot of me, don't worry. We're going to have to work out a way of life that makes it possible for us to spend plenty of time together.' He put a hand under her chin and turned her face up towards him. 'Starting now...'

'Sure you don't want lunch first?' she mocked.

'You're the first course.' Nick's teeth softly nibbled her ear. 'Mmm...delicious.' His mouth moved down her cheek and found her lips; his hands moved too, a groan of pleasure escaped her as they strayed from her breasts downward, slowly caressing and exploring. Nick's breathing thickened. 'Darling...' he muttered, his face buried on her body. 'Oh, God, Gina, if you knew how much I want you...'

She did know; she wanted him as much, moaning with need, her back arching to meet him as he moved against her, inside her at last, their bodies merging into one slow, pulsing, agonising rhythm, a crescendo of satisfaction.

They were married in early June on a day which began with a thunderstorm, at around dawn, but broke out into brilliant sunshine just as Gina arrived at St Margaret's, Westminster Abbey, in a beribboned white Rolls-Royce. Although she and Nick were getting married in one of London's most fashionable churches it was not a society wedding. Almost everyone in the congregation knew them well, and most of the guests at the reception later either worked at the *Sentinel* or for one of Caspian International's other newspapers.

Gina had asked Des Amery to stand in for her father, and give her away. 'I just got over the ordeal of giving Roz away!' he had said, shuddering. 'One of the most nerve-racking jobs I've ever done, let me tell you!'

'You should be an expert at it now, then,' said Gina, amused, then gave him a pleading look. 'And really, Des...I don't have anyone else old enough to be my father to walk down the aisle with me! I've known you longer than anyone else, too, remember.'

He had given in, then, although he'd kicked a little at the idea of wearing morning dress. Daniel had made him wear morning dress, too. Roz and Daniel had had a very formal wedding, in France, crowded with French relatives, old men up from the country in their best clothes, their wives in flowery hats, quarrelling children everywhere. It had been great fun, and the food had, naturally, been fabulous. Gina had been Roz's bridesmaid, and now Roz and Hazel were her matrons of honour, both wearing a ravishing shade of kingfisher-blue and carrying bouquets of cream roses and carnations.

Gina had decided against wearing a white dress, as this was her second marriage. She chose a creamy ivory satin, designed by one of Paris's top couturiers in an elegant style beautifully cut for the absolute maximum of effect on her slender figure. The bodice didn't cling, it fell smoothly from a scooped-out neckline, over her high breasts; the long sleeves flared out at the elbow, like the throats of cream Arum lilies, half-covering her hands. Her waist was ignored, the material floated on over it to her hips, giving her a freedom to move which emphasised her sleek and feminine figure.

'Nervous?' Des asked her, taking her hand and drawing it through his arm as they began the slow walk down the aisle of St Margaret's to the triumphant music of the organ.

Gina nodded, swallowing. She was trembling and wondering if she would ever make it to the altar.

'We all survive it, don't worry,' said Des, but she looked ahead with dread, down the aisle of the sixteenth-century church, with its astonishing modern stained glass by John Piper, seeing the distance to the altar like a long, long tunnel. Nerves closed her throat up. Then, at the end there was Nick, turning to look at her, and Gina felt strength flooding back into her.

It had been a long journey from the moment they first met on the windswept wintry building site on which Barbary Wharf now stood, to this moment now, where they would stand together at the altar to be joined in holy matrimony. She had never imagined they would end up here. In fact, it had been touch and go at times that she wouldn't push Nick out of one of the penthouse windows. But they were here, and she had never in her life felt so sure about anything as she was about loving him.

He had asked Piet to be his best man; just as Gina had asked Hazel to be her matron of honour.

'Can't you find a job for Nicky to do?' Hazel had asked, laughing as she nursed her baby last night. She and Piet were staying with Gina in her apartment, and the baby had woken up several times during the night, waking Gina, too. 'Sorry about this,' Hazel had said, distracted and red-eyed as she fed her infant for the second time. 'The night before your wedding too! You need your beauty sleep; it's a shame. We should have spent the night at a hotel.'

'I wasn't asleep,' Gina had assured her. 'I've been tossing and turning all night. Nicky didn't wake me up.' She had watched the flushed little face at Hazel's breast, aching with envy. 'He is gorgeous, Hazel—you are lucky. I want to start a family right away, but I'm not sure how Nick feels. He has just made me chairman of the board of directors and I work horribly long hours, now that I'm running the *Sentinel*. I've only seen him at weekends lately; I hope that isn't going to be the pattern after we're married.'

Hazel had detached her baby from herself and hoisted him over her shoulder, patting his back. She'd given Gina one of her firm, direct looks. 'Talk to Nick frankly, tell him you want to start a family. He can't know until you tell him.'

Gina hadn't yet. It could wait until they were on their honeymoon and alone all the time.

They had picked a simple, modern version of the wedding ceremony, too, and in a surprisingly short time they had exchanged vows and rings, kissed each other, and gone into the vestry to sign the register, along with Nick's sisters and mother, his brother-in-law and a handful of other invited witnesses.

Gina had been hugged by Alessa and Lilith, Nick's elder sister, and Mrs Caspian, who had tears in her eyes.
'It was a lovely wedding! I'm so happy, Gina!'

'Then why are you crying, Mama?' Nick had teased.

When they were on their way back to Barbary Wharf for the huge reception which was being given at the Barbary Wharf hotel, Nick leaned back, groaning, balancing his top hat on his knee.

'I'm exhausted. This has been the longest day of my life so far. And it isn't even half over yet!'

'Changed your mind about marrying me already, Nick?' Gina asked, and he gave her a glittering smile.

'For that you get kissed until you scream!'

Laughing with alarm, she protested, 'No, Nick, mind my head-dress and my hair and...'

The rest was swallowed up into passionate darkness, and with her eyes shut she put an arm around his neck and murmured huskily under his mouth.

'Oh, Nick...Nick...'

The car slowed as they approached the Barbary Wharf complex and Nick sat upright, very flushed, straightening his grey silk cravat and picking up his top hat from the floor.

'Well, here we go again!'

Representatives from all departments of the *Sentinel* staff had been invited: from the editor, Fabien Arnaud, down to one of the ladies who cleaned the offices early each morning before the staff arrived.

Even the Torelli family had been invited—Mrs Torelli and her two sons and their wives. Tony Torelli and his wife Angela had had to refuse as they were spending the whole of the summer in Sicily, their first long holiday in years. Roberto had accepted and was bringing his wife, Sandra, whom Mrs Torelli detested so much that she had run out to catch Gina, on her way across the plaza, a few weeks ago, to complain.

'Why you invite Sandra? Big mistake, she is bad trouble.'

'I couldn't invite Roberto without her,' Gina had gently pointed out, but Mrs Torelli didn't care about wedding etiquette.

'You wait and see, she is very stupid, terrible taste— I shall pretend I don't know her.'

Talking to Roz and Sophie over lunch that week, Gina had said, 'Actually, I invited Sandra because I can't wait to see her and find out if she is as bad as Mamma Torelli says!'

'I expect she is!' Roz had cynically said. 'She's a shrewd old bird.'

Gina had spent weeks planning the big day: choosing a menu, arranging for musicians, buying new outfits for her honeymoon. One of the toughest jobs was drawing up the guest list, because they couldn't invite everyone but anyone who was left out was going to be upset.

She and Nick welcomed them at the door, shaking hands with everyone who arrived. Faces began to swim past Gina, not all of them familiar to her. Apart from his own family, Nick had invited many friends whom she had never met, although some of them she knew very well indeed.

Roz's half-sister, Irena, had flown back from Spain with her husband Esteban, once marketing director of the *Sentinel*. Irena looked older than she had last time Gina saw her: marriage had matured her delicate features but that she was happy there was no question, and Esteban looked like a very contented man.

'We're almost sisters now that your father has given me away!' Gina told Irena, laughing.

'He knows the routine by heart,' Irena agreed. 'First me, then Roz, and now you! He looked very dignified and very unhappy, in his morning suit, didn't he? Poor Des, he feels much more at home in old jeans and a sweater.'

'Can you recommend married life?' asked Gina, and Irena gave her a shy, smiling nod.

'We're holding up the queue, Irena,' Esteban pointed out with his grave concern for doing things properly, and Irena smiled at him, ruefully, then kissed Gina on both cheeks.

'So we are. See you later. Be happy, Gina!'

Esteban kissed her just as formally, his dark eyes kind. 'You make an enchanting bride!'

Gina had no relatives of her own, but although she had felt sad about that at first she had comforted herself by inviting all her friends, from the *Sentinel*. Sophie, who, of course, came with her husband, Guy Faulkner, from the legal department, and Valerie Collingwood, who was now one of their leading women writers and making a really big name for herself in Fleet Street. She had come with her husband, Gilbey Collingwood, an ex-accountant who worked on the business section of the paper. For a long time Sophie and Valerie had been icily hostile to each other, over Gib, but today they were the best of friends.

Gina later saw them sitting together during the reception lunch, laughing and talking as they ate the excellent food which Gina had chosen. The wine had all been picked by Nick.

On the same table and looking radiantly happy was the beautiful dark-haired Molly, wife of famous actor Mac Cameron, whose threatened libel suit had given Nick some bad nights last year. Gina had invited them because she had become very fond of Molly during the period when the *Sentinel* was running stories about her and the baby she claimed was Mac's, and she liked Mac, too. Today, he looked brown and relaxed, and very sexy in his Armani suit, managing to look ten years younger since his marriage and the discovery that he was a father. He had always had a supple body and amazing presence but happiness had given him a new glow.

Opposite him, she noticed, sat Colette Tse. At the sight of her, Gina's smiled stiffened.

'We must invite Colette, you know,' Nick had drily said, glancing down her first draft of the guest list.

'Oh, yes, of course, how could I forget her?' Gina had given him a sweet smile at which he laughed wickedly, perfectly aware of why she had omitted Colette's name.

'Darling, she is writing this biography; she has to be invited on that count alone, not to mention the fact that she is features editor and you've invited all of the other heads of department. It would be noticed if she was left out.'

Gina took the list and wrote in Colette's name.

'You don't really mind inviting her, do you?' Nick asked uncertainly and she shook her head, her smile rueful.

'No, the hostility is all on Colette's side, not mine.' Whenever she met Colette around the newspaper offices she felt the icy wind of the other woman's dislike.

She had known all along that in the end she would have to invite her to the wedding, but she was afraid Colette would somehow manage to spoil the day for her. Just having her there, at the reception, even with all those hundreds of other guests, made Gina uneasy.

Colette had been in the moving line of people they had shaken hands with at the door but Gina had not had to do more than smile and say, 'Thank you for coming.' Colette had not given her a chance to say anything else, she had murmured something polite and walked on, looking elegantly sophisticated in a glowing dark red silk dress. She was strikingly lovely, with her straight black hair and slanting eyes, her golden-olive skin.

Gina glanced at the man sitting next to her and recognised him—one of the reporters, the blond man who had often been seen with Colette over the last few months. Was their relationship serious, wondered Gina, or was she hoping too much?

Leaning over, at that moment, Roz with a wicked smile whispered, 'Is that the famous Sandra?'

Gina followed her eyes to a table on the other side of the room. A very curvaceous woman with obviously dyed red hair in a tight green satin dress was grabbing a waiter's arm as he passed, gesticulating wildly.

'Yes, that's her. Mamma Torelli knew what she was talking about, just as you suspected. Poor Roberto.'

'I'd say he's crazy about her,' murmured Roz. 'She's certainly got sex appeal, even if it comes in a gaudy package. Don't you think so, Nick?'

Nick glanced across the room and his mouth twisted. 'Well, not to my taste, but I suppose she might attract men who like their sex very blatantly advertised. I'm not surprised Mrs Torelli doesn't like her—they're very different types.'

'Mrs Torelli might forgive her if she came up with a grandchild,' Gina said, looking at him through her lashes.

Nick's mother became interested. 'She doesn't look as if she ever will, either, does she? That's very sad. Every woman wants grandchildren. I hope I'm going to get some from you now, Nick, before I'm too old to enjoy them.'

'Give us a chance, we only got married today,' he protested.

'Well, don't delay too long,' his mother firmly told him.

'We won't,' Gina promised her and Nick threw her a wry, smiling sideways glance.

'Oh, won't we? I thought you were a career woman? What happens to your career if you have a baby?'

'I shall have them both,' Gina said. 'It will take some juggling and careful planning but I don't see why I shouldn't have a baby and a career.'

'I don't remember discussing this,' Nick said, brows arching. 'Was it a one-woman decision, or am I allowed a point of view?'

'We'll talk about it tonight,' she said, flushed but emboldened by the approval in his mother's smile.

'We won't,' Nick said. 'Tonight, we'll be much too busy to do any talking.'

Gina's skin heated as laughter went around the table, then she met Nick's passionate grey eyes and her breath caught. For a second everyone else in the room seemed to vanish and they were alone, desire beating between them like a flame. It had been a long, long journey but at last they had overcome all the barriers between them; all the anger and hatred and grief had gone. I am so happy, she thought. Please, let this last forever.

HARLEQUIN PRESENTS®

Coming Next Month

"BARBARY WHARF" SWEEPSTAKES
OFFICIAL RULES — NO PURCHASE NECESSARY

1. To enter each drawing complete the appropriate Offical Entry Form. Alternatively, you may enter any drawing by hand printing on a 3" × 5" card (mechanical reproductions are not acceptable) your name, address, daytime telephone number and prize for which that entry is being submitted (Wedgwood Tea Set, $1,000 Shopping Spree, Sterling Silver Candelabras, Royal Doulton China, Crabtree & Evelyn Gift Baskets or Sterling Silver Tray) and mailing it to: Barbary Wharf Sweepstakes, P.O. Box 1397, Buffalo, NY 14269-1397.

No responsibility is assumed for lost, late or misdirected mail. For eligibility all entries must be sent separately with first class postage affixed and be received by 11/23/92 for Wedgwood Tea Set (approx. value $543) or, at winner's option, $500 cash drawing; 12/22/92 for the $1,000 Shopping Spree at any retail establishment winner selects or, at winner's option, $1,000 cash drawing; 1/22/93 for Sterling Silver Candelabras (approx. value $875) or, at winner's option, $700 cash drawing, 2/22/93 for the Royal Doulton China service for 8 (approx. value $1,060) or, at winner's option, $900 cash drawing; 3/22/93 for the 12 monthly Crabtree & Evelyn Gift Baskets (approx. value $960) or, at winner's option, $750 cash drawing and, 4/22/93 for the Sterling Silver Tray (approx. value $1,200) or, at winner's option, $750 cash drawing. All winners will be selected in random drawings to be held within 7 days of each drawing eligibility deadline.

A random drawing from amongst all eligible entries received for participation in any or all drawings will be held no later than April 29, 1993 to award the Grand Prize of a 10 day trip for two (2) to London, England (approx. value $6,000) or, at winner's option, $6,000 cash. Travel option includes 10 nights accommodation at the Kensington Park Hotel, Continental breakfast daily, theater tickets for 2, plus round trip airfare and $1,000 spending money; air transportation is from commercial airport nearest winner's home; travel must be completed within 12 months of winner notification, and is subject to space and accommodation availability; travellers must sign and return a Release of Liability prior to traveling.

2. Sweepstakes offer is open only to residents of the U.S. (except Puerto Rico), and Canada who are 21 years of age or older, except employees and immediate family members of Torstar Corp., its affiliates, subsidiaries, and all agencies, entities and persons connected with the use, marketing, or conduct of this sweepstakes. All federal, state, provincial, municipal and local laws apply. Offer void wherever prohibited by law. Taxes and/or duties are the sole responsibility of the winner. Any litigation within the province of Quebec respecting the conduct and awarding of a prize may be submitted to the Régie des loteries et courses du Quebec. All prizes will be awarded; winners will be notified by mail. No substitution of prizes is permitted. Winner selection is under the supervision of D.L. Blair, Inc., an independent judging organization whose decisions are final. Chances of winning in any drawing are dependent upon the number of eligible entries received. All prizes are valued in U.S. currency.

3. Potential winners must sign and return an Affidavit of Eligibility within 30 days of notification. In the event of non-compliance within this time period, the prize may be awarded to an alternate winner. Any prize or prize notification returned as undeliverable may result in the awarding of that prize to an alternate winner. By acceptance of their prize, winners consent to the use of their names, photographs or their likenesses for purposes of advertising, trade and promotion on behalf of Torstar Corp. without further compensation to the winner unless prohibited by law. Canadian winners must correctly answer a time-limited arithmetical question in order to be awarded a prize.

4. For a list of winners (available after 5/31/93), send a separate stamped, self-addressed envelope to: Barbary Wharf Sweepstakes Winners, P.O. Box 4526, Blair, NE 68009.

This month's special prize:

A Reed & Barton Tray of Sterling Silver!

If you're the winner of this prize, you and your family will own a precious heirloom you'll cherish always—a sterling silver tray from Reed & Barton! This 15″ long oval tray is made of solid silver in the classic Chippendale pattern; it will add a note of beauty and elegance to any setting.

The Grand Prize:
An English Holiday for Two!

Visit London and tour the neighborhoods where the characters in *Barbary Wharf* work and fall in love. Visit the fabulous shops, the museums, the Tower of London and Buckingham Palace...enjoy theater and fine dining. And as part of your ten-day holiday, you'll be invited to lunch with the author, Charlotte Lamb! Round-trip airfare for two, first-class hotels, and meals are all included.

BARBARY WHARF
SWEEPSTAKES
OFFICIAL
ENTRY FORM

THIS MONTH'S SPECIAL PRIZE:

Reed & Barton Silver Tray

NOTICE » Entry must be received by April 22, 1993.
Winner will be notified by April 30, 1993.

GRAND PRIZE:

A Vacation to England!

See prize descriptions on the back of this entry form.

Fill in your name and address below and return this
entry form with your invoice in the reply envelope provided.
Good luck!

NAME

ADDRESS

CITY   STATE/PROV.   ZIP/POSTAL CODE

(   )

DAYTIME PHONE NUMBER   (AREA CODE)

BW-M6